<u>What Kids Say About Carole Marsh Mysteries . . .</u>

I love the real locations! Reading the book always makes me want to go and visit them all on our next family vacation. My Mom says maybe, but I can't wait!

One day, I want to be a real kid in one of Ms. Marsh's mystery books. I think it would be fun, and I think I am a real character anyway. I filled out the application and sent it in and am keeping my fingers crossed!

History was not my favorite subject till I starting reading Carole Marsh Mysteries. Ms. Marsh really brings history to life. Also, she leaves room for the scary and fun.

I think Christina is so smart and br~~a~~ She i~~s~~ ~~luc~~~~ky to b~~ mystery books because she gets to go ~~—~~ ~~er~~ just how much of the book is true a~~~~ figure that out is fun!

Grant is cool and funny! He makes ~~me laugh a lot!!~~

I like that there are boys and girls in the story of different ages. Some mysteries I outgrow, but I can always find a favorite character to identify with in these books.

They are scary, but not too scary. They are funny. I learn a lot. There is always food which makes me hungry. I feel like I am there.

<u>What Adults Say About Carole Marsh Mysteries . . .</u>

I think kids love these books because they have such a wealth of detail. I know I learn a lot reading them! It's an engaging way to look at the history of any place or event. I always say I'm only going to read one chapter to the kids, but that never happens—it's always two or three, at least!   —Librarian

Reading the mystery and going on the field trip—Scavenger Hunt in hand—was the most fun our class ever had! It really brought the place and its history to life. They loved the real kids characters and all the humor. I loved seeing them learn that reading is an experience to enjoy!   —4th grade teacher

Carole Marsh is really on to something with these unique mysteries. They are so clever; kids want to read them all. The Teacher's Guides are chock full of activities, recipes, and additional fascinating information. My kids thought I was an expert on the subject—and with this tool, I felt like it!   —3rd grade teacher

My students loved writing their own Real Kids/Real Places mystery book! Ms. Marsh's reproducible guidelines are a real jewel. They learned about copyright and more & ended up with their own book they were so proud of!   —Reading/Writing Teacher

The Mystery on the
CALIFORNIA
MISSION TRAIL

CAROLE MARSH MYSTERIES

by
Carole Marsh

Published by Gallopade International/Carole Marsh Books. Printed in the United States of America.

Editorial Assistant: Michele Yother

Cover design: Vicki DeJoy; Editor: Jenny Corsey; Graphic Design: Steve St. Laurent; Layout and footer design: Lynette Rowe; Photography: Amanda McCutcheon.

Also available:
The Mystery on the California Mission Trail Teacher's Guide
1,000 Readers - Father Junípero Serra

Gallopade is proud to be a member of these educational organizations and associations:

The National School Supply and Equipment Association
Association for Supervision and Curriculum Development
The National Council for the Social Studies
Museum Store Association
Association of Partners for Public Lands

This book is dedicated to the real Mimi and Papa, who are every bit as cool and adventurous in real life as in this book.

– *MY*

This book is a complete work of fiction. All events are fictionalized, and although the first names of real children are used, their characterization in this book is fiction.

Readers: Please watch for each mission's seal in the footers throughout the story.

For additional information on Carole Marsh Mysteries, visit: www.carolemarshmysteries.com

Are we going to get in trouble for this?

20 YEARS AGO . . .

As a mother and an author, one of the fondest periods of my life was when I decided to write mystery books for children. At this time (1979) kids were pretty much glued to the TV, something parents and teachers complained about the way they do about video games today.

I decided to set each mystery in a real place—a place kids could go and visit for themselves after reading the book. And I also used real children as characters. Usually a couple of my own children served as characters, and I had no trouble recruiting kids from the book's location to also be characters.

Also, I wanted all the kids—boys and girls of all ages—to participate in solving the mystery. And, I wanted kids to learn something as they read. Something about the history of the location. And I wanted the stories to be funny.

That formula of real+scary+smart+fun served me well. The kids and I had a great time visiting each site and many of the events in the stories actually came out of our experiences there. (For example, we really did experience an earthquake while visiting one of the missions!)

I love getting letters from teachers and parents who say they read the book with their class or child, then visited the historic site and saw all the places in the mystery for themselves. What's so great about that? What's great is that you and your children have an experience that bonds you together forever. Something you shared. Something you both cared about at the time. Something that crossed all age levels—a good story, a good scare, a good laugh!

20 years later,

Carole Marsh

Christina Yother **Grant Yother** **Shelly Avillo** **Allison Avillo**

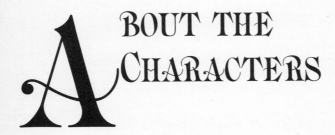

ABOUT THE CHARACTERS

Christina Yother, 9, from Peachtree City, Georgia

Grant Yother, 7, from Peachtree City, Georgia
Christina's brother

Shelly Avillo as Maria, 12, from Lompoc, California, near
Mission La Purísima Concepción

Allison Avillo as Clara, 10, Maria's sister

The many places featured in the book actually exist and are
worth a visit! Perhaps you could read the book and follow the
trail these kids went on during their mysterious adventure!

Titles in the Carole Marsh Mysteries Series

Books and Teacher's Guides are available at booksellers, libraries, school supply stores, museums, and many other locations!

CONTENTS

1 A NEW MYSTERY

Christina and Grant stared at the black and white pieces of the chess game they were playing. Christina's hand hovered just inches over the board while they motionlessly listened to Mimi's phone conversation.

"California missions? Mystery? Sounds exciting. We'll fly out immediately," they heard Mimi say.

Christina, 9, a fourth-grader in Peachtree City, Georgia and her brother Grant, 7, ran into the kitchen where their grandmother Mimi had just hung up the phone. The smell of fudgy brownies filled the air.

"Where Mimi? Where are we going this time?" Christina asked, looking up expectantly.

"What?" asked Mimi, looking at her grandchildren with a smile. "You two weren't eavesdropping again, were you?"

California . . .
Missions?

Where Are
We Going?

Grant and Christina tried to look apologetic, but their bright blue eyes gave away their excited anticipation of where they might be going.

"We're going to California," said Mimi, "and we've got to leave tomorrow. My mission mystery has to be written by July."

Grant looked at Christina and shrugged his shoulders. They were both used to Mimi's indecipherable comments. Their grandmother was not like any of the other grandmothers they knew. She had bright blond hair, wrote mystery books, and took off on adventures at a moment's notice. The best part was she always took them along too!

"What's your mission, Mimi?" asked Grant.

"What?" asked Mimi, as she rubbed Grant's short blond hair in confusion. "Oh, not *my* mission—California missions! In the 1700s and 1800s, Spanish *padres*, or priests, built a chain of 21 missions along 600 miles of the California coastline. The missions are churches, but they're also more. In addition to the church, missions included living quarters for the *padres* and the Indians they converted to Christianity, plus everything they needed to survive. Mission grounds included farmland, vineyards, stables, herds of cattle and sheep,

Where Are
We Going?

To California!

and gardens.

"Today, the missions are open to visitors who come to tour the restored buildings and view the ancient artifacts, golden statues, and elaborate altars. Missions are an important part of California's history."

"Why are we going to see them?" Christina asked.

"California's missions are the setting for my next mystery book," Mimi replied. "The old adobe and stone buildings with all their Spanish arches and orange tile roofs will be a great backdrop to some scary adventures!"

Grant looked up at Mimi with a grin. "*Maybeee* there's gold in them thar hills!" he exclaimed.

"Oh, brother," said Christina, rolling her eyes. She was used to Grant's silly sayings and songs. In fact, she had plenty of her own. Obviously he knew California was famous for the Gold Rush. He had always been interested in any kind of search for treasure.

"How long will we be there, Mimi?" Christina asked in her most serious and mature voice.

"That depends on how long it takes to solve the mystery," Mimi answered mysteriously.

"Uh, oh," Christina thought. Mimi made that

To California!

What Are Missions?

sound so easy. But Christina recalled all the spooky trouble that Mimi could get them all into on any of her mystery book writing adventures–or misadventures, as Christina preferred to call them.

What Are
Missions?

To The Airport
Tomorrow!

2 CALIFORNIA, HERE WE COME!

Christina and Grant sat in seats 14B and 14A on the newly remodeled 747 Delta airplane.

Christina buckled her seatbelt and pulled the strap tight. She reached over to Grant in the window seat next to her and pulled his seatbelt tight, too.

"Ouch," cried Grant. "I can't breathe!"

Christina ignored his complaints. She liked to fly, but she always got butterflies in her stomach just before take-off. She started arranging her books, paper, pens, and headphones in the pocket in front of her.

Grant pulled out his *California Pocket Guide* and began quizzing Christina on California state facts.

"What's the state tree?" he asked. "The California redwood," he immediately answered. "What's the state flower?" he asked. "The golden poppy," he replied before

Ready To
Take Off?

California
Trivia

Christina could respond.

"Hey, listen to this," he said, flipping to another page in his book. "The state animal is the California grizzly bear, but there are no more wild grizzlies left in California! The last one died in 1922. Awww, I guess that means we won't get to see any."

"Only on the state flag," replied Christina.

Grant flipped to the state flag page in his book and nodded.

"Ah, the state song," he said, after turning the page again. "I LOVE YOU CALIFORNIA, YOU'RE THE GREATEST STATE OF ALL," his voice rang out, as Christina slid low in her seat from embarrassment.

"Sshhh!" Christina hissed to Grant, snatching the book out of his hands. She flipped through the pages while Grant leaned down and pulled a baggie, that looked like it was stuffed full of dirt, out of his carry-on bag.

Mimi leaned over from the seat across the aisle and handed each of them a pack of M&Ms.

"Thnnnkks Mmmmi," mumbled Grant, already chewing on one of the brownies Mimi had baked yesterday.

Papa walked down the aisle with an overstuffed carry-on bag. He carried three cameras, two laptop computers, and a mess of cables that kept Mimi, and now

California
Trivia

Aahh.
M&Ms!

Christina too, connected to the Internet wherever they went.

Mimi always took her computer for writing, and now Christina had her own laptop too. She had persuaded Papa to bring it along even though it was one more thing to keep up with. He knew she especially wanted to bring it for this trip. Besides using her favorite art and design programs, she wanted to e-mail her friends back in Peachtree City. She loved going on trips with Mimi and Papa, but she did miss hearing what all her friends were doing. She had gotten really close to the eight girls in her Girl Scout troop and planned to e-mail them all every day!

Papa gave Christina a big grin as he stuffed the carry-on bag into the overhead compartment. "In my opinion, these seats are just too darn close," he said. Papa always had opinions, and even though she couldn't ever get completely used to his gruff way of expressing them, Christina had learned that she usually agreed with him.

Just before sitting down, Papa leaned over and handed Grant a bright red canvas backpack. "Uncle Michael said you might need this," Papa said.

Christina looked curiously at the backpack and tried to guess what was inside. Uncle Michael was always giving Grant weird, neat stuff that seemed to come in handy

Aahh,
M&Ms!

Something
for Grant

sooner or later. Christina leaned over a little more to see what was inside, but Grant turned towards the window to keep the contents hidden from view.

He unzipped the pocket, peeked inside, and doubled over in laughter.

Something for
Grant . . .

That's funny!

3 JOHN WAYNE AIRPORT

The plane touched down at the John Wayne Airport in Orange County, California.

"In my opinion, this sure beats fighting the zoo at the L.A. airport," said Papa, looking around the small airport terminal.

"Hey, there's Big John!" he exclaimed.

"Who's Big John?" Christina asked, looking around for someone she might recognize.

"John Wayne," Papa replied, walking over to a large bronze statue of the legendary actor of cowboy movie fame.

"John Wayne looks pretty tough," said Grant, as he circled around the statue. "Papa, he reminds me of you!"

Papa laughed and swatted Grant on the bottom in jest. "Let's go!" he said.

Christina and Grant wheeled their suitcases

Orange County,
California

Through The
Airport

through the airport as they followed Mimi and Papa through the crowd. Christina's suitcase was a pretty shade of lavender, her favorite color. Grant's bag was decorated with superheroes. "At least they're easy to spot," Papa always said. In his opinion, his grandkids' luggage was gaudy.

"I'm hungry," moaned Christina, as she paused to switch her suitcase to her other hand.

"You ate non-stop on the plane!" said Mimi, dismissing Christina's complaint. She knew Christina had spotted the flashing neon pizza sign up ahead. Just the *idea* of pizza had a tendency to make Christina's tummy growl loud enough for anyone to hear.

Grant smirked at his sister, chocolate brownie crumbs still smudged across his cheek. But when he saw the pizza sign, his stomach grumbled and he mumbled a quiet "me too."

"Hurry up, Grant," Christina called over her shoulder, as she slowed down a little.

Grant's legs worked fast to keep up. He was a little small for his age, but that wasn't why he was falling behind now. He stopped at an exhibit case labeled CALIFORNIA GOLD! He looked from one end to the other at the Gold Rush artifacts on display, a pea-size gold nugget in the

Through The
Airport

Look. . .
Gold!

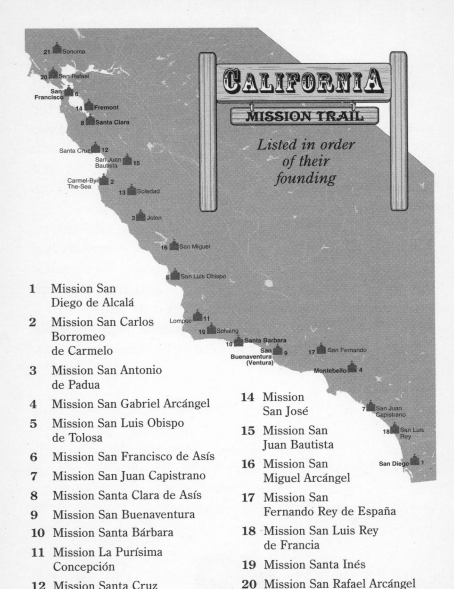

CALIFORNIA

MISSION TRAIL

Listed in order of their founding

21 Sonoma
20 San Rafael
San Francisco 6.
14 Fremont
8 Santa Clara
Santa Cruz 12
San Juan Bautista 15
Carmel-By-The-Sea 2
13 Soledad
3 Jolon
16 San Miguel
5 San Luis Obispo
Lompoc 11
19 Solvang
10 Santa Barbara
San Buenaventura (Ventura) 9
17 San Fernando
Montebello 4
7 San Juan Capistrano
18 San Luis Rey
San Diego 1

1 Mission San Diego de Alcalá

2 Mission San Carlos Borromeo de Carmelo

3 Mission San Antonio de Padua

4 Mission San Gabriel Arcángel

5 Mission San Luis Obispo de Tolosa

6 Mission San Francisco de Asís

7 Mission San Juan Capistrano

8 Mission Santa Clara de Asís

9 Mission San Buenaventura

10 Mission Santa Bárbara

11 Mission La Purísima Concepción

12 Mission Santa Cruz

13 Mission Nuestra Señora de la Soledad

14 Mission San José

15 Mission San Juan Bautista

16 Mission San Miguel Arcángel

17 Mission San Fernando Rey de España

18 Mission San Luis Rey de Francia

19 Mission Santa Inés

20 Mission San Rafael Arcángel

21 Mission San Francisco de Sonoma

middle.

"Look at that," he said to Christina. "That's the size of the gold nugget James Marshall found in 1848 that started the California Gold Rush! It sure doesn't look very big."

Grant realized everyone was gone, and he was talking to himself.

"Yikes!" he said, as he grabbed his suitcase and headed to the transportation area at a run. He spotted Christina's worried face looking for him and ran to catch up.

"Wait up!" Christina hollered, as Grant ran right past her to where Mimi and Papa were standing.

Suddenly a dark-haired man stalked up to them and snatched Mimi's suitcase right out of her hand!

4 MISSION LA PURÍSIMA

"I'll take that bag for you," the strange man said.

"John!" exclaimed Mimi, giving the man a big hug. "It's *wonderful* to see you again!"

Papa visibly relaxed. Christina thought Papa had been ready to grab hold of this John guy, just like John had grabbed hold of Mimi's suitcase. In fact, Christina was sure he had been!

Mimi introduced everyone, explaining how she and John had met years before when Mimi was autographing her *California Big Activity Book for Kids* at the Northern California Book Show.

"John has written several adult books about the California missions," said Mimi. "Besides being a ranger at one of the missions, he's also on the Board of Directors that oversees the preservation and operation of all the

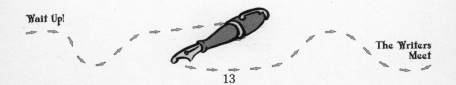

Wait Up!

The Writers Meet

13

California mission sites."

"It's a full-time job, what with 21 missions stretching up and down the coast of California, practically from the Mexican border all the way up to the Sonoma Valley, north of San Francisco Bay," John said good-naturedly. "When the idea of a children's mystery came up at one of our meetings, there was no way I could tackle that job too. Besides, I knew this lady was the perfect author for the book!

"By the way," John added, looking at Christina. "My daughters are planning to go with us while I take all of you around to visit each mission. Maria is 12 and Clara is 11, and they're very anxious to meet you."

"Well, c'mon," said Mimi. "Let's get this show on the road!"

They all piled into a big silver Lincoln Navigator that was parked along the curb outside the Ground Transportation sign.

"You can't leave your car on the curb at Atlanta's Hartsfield International Airport," said Papa, referring to the world's busiest airport, where they had flown out of earlier that morning. "In fact, nowadays you're lucky if they let you slow down to a complete stop while your passengers get in!"

The Writers
Meet

To La
Purisima

During the drive to Mission La Purísima, which was near where John and his family lived, John described the California missions.

"The central focus of each mission is the church," he explained. "The missions were founded to instruct the early inhabitants of the land in the Catholic faith. The California Indians were to become Neophytes (newly baptized Catholics), to learn Spanish, and to work at the missions. Building missions was a way to get new citizens and land for Spain.

"Missionaries and soldiers traveled together so both a mission and a *presidio*, or fort, were built," John continued. "They had a hard time as they made their way into California. They got lost. They died from scurvy and other diseases because they lacked healthy food. And they suffered bad weather, heat, and exhaustion. In fact, many times, two expeditions were sent to the same place—one by land and one by sea. That way, if one group got lost or perished, which was fairly likely back then, there was still a chance the other group would make it."

"Did the Indians like the new missions?" Christina asked.

"At first, the Indians did not know what to make of the strangers," John said. "They wandered around the new

To La Purisima

Some Mission History

mission, often stealing whatever they could carry. Father Junípero Serra, who helped found the first missions, believed the mission should continue to try to make friends with the Indians, but the soldiers did not. The soldiers killed many Indians. Eventually, the mission and the *presidio* were separated to keep them from killing the Indians. But after Indians attacked the unprotected mission, the mission moved back to the safety of the *presidio*. This same pattern was repeated at other missions."

When they pulled up at Mission La Purísima, Grant and Christina stared wide-eyed out the Navigator's windows. All around them were gardens and orchards and animals and people who looked as if they were transported out of a scene from hundreds of years ago! In the middle of all this activity stood a long adobe church covered in red clay roof tiles. A few small, arched windows dotted the side of the building. A taller section of wall on one end had three openings where three bells should have hung. A cross topped the roof above the empty bell alcoves.

Mimi laughed at the kids' astonished expressions, and said, "Get out and explore, you two. See what California mission life was like 200+ years ago!"

Christina and Grant slid out of the vehicle. As soon

Some Mission History

Mission La Purísima

as they landed on the ground, two dark-haired girls waved and ran up to them.

"Hi, Christina! Hi, Grant!" the girls said together.

"I'm Maria, and this is my sister Clara," said the slightly taller girl.

"Maria and Clara are excited to have visitors," said John. "We don't get too many kids here that stay for more than a one-day visit, do we?" he asked, looking fondly at his daughters.

Each girl smiled and shook her head at their Dad, then turned back to Christina and Grant. "Do you want to meet the docents?" asked Clara.

"They're the people in costume," explained Maria. "We can watch them spin and weave wool and make candles. Grant, you'd like the blacksmith shop, I'll bet," she added.

Grant and Christina turned and looked at Mimi, who gave them a little nod. "Sure," Christina said, and they all four turned and jogged across the field. Suddenly Grant turned and ran back to the car. He leaned into the backseat and grabbed the red backpack that Uncle Michael had given him. He hooked the straps across his shoulders and ran back to catch up with the girls.

Maria chattered non-stop, and Clara nodded her

head vigorously as they took Christina and Grant on a tour of the mission.

"This is the most completely restored mission in California," said Maria. "After the earthquake of 1812, not a single building was standing! But the California Conservation Corps built it back just like the original, and now it's a state park."

"Our Dad is a ranger here, and we live in a *casa* right across the street," Clara said proudly.

Grant and Christina explored the mission with Maria and Clara as their own personal tour guides for the rest of the afternoon. When Grant ran off to explore the path along the water storage pools and fields on his own, he noticed several big shoe prints with a distinctive wavy line across the tread.

"I must have mystery on the brain," he said to himself, dismissing the inkling of dread tingling through his spine.

A few minutes later Grant caught back up with the girls, and they all went across the street to find the adults at the sprawling house where Maria and Clara lived. They walked into a big open living room with long wooden beams that stretched across the width of the ceiling. Colorful Mexican art painted from a palette of bright blues, bold

Mission La
Purisima

Maria &
Clara's Casa

yellows, warm reds, and lush greens decorated the walls.

Still standing in the doorway and looking over Grant's head, Christina spotted Mimi sitting on a big, overstuffed, cream-colored sofa. Christina knew from one glance at Mimi's expression that something was terribly wrong!

Maria &
Clara's Casa

Something's
Wrong!

5 QUEEN OF THE MISSIONS

Christina continued to look at Mimi as they walked into the big open room. Christina forced a smile at Mimi, as she glanced around at the other adults. Christina's chest tightened when Mimi didn't smile back reassuringly, as she usually did.

Mimi and Papa sat across from a woman in a beautiful, authentic, Spanish-style dress and two men in jeans and work shirts. John paced in a circle around the group, anger turning his tan face bright red.

"I can't believe someone would steal the bells," sobbed the woman.

"That's our Mama," Clara said to Christina and Grant softly. "Her name is Rosario."

Mimi glanced towards the door at the kids and noticed Christina's worried face. Christina was tugging on

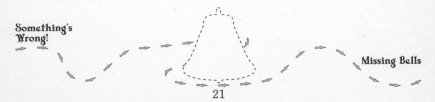

Something's Wrong!

Missing Bells

21

her ear like she always did when she was upset, which was any time Mimi or Papa were upset.

"Let's notify the police, and then we need to get these children some dinner," said Mimi to the adults before she turned back to give a reassuring smile to the kids.

"Children, take your bags to your room. Hurry so we can eat soon," said Mimi, and the kids got busy.

"Do you think I can check e-mail?" asked Christina.

"Nope. I'm STARVED!" he replied, with a grin.

"Well I can get it set up," Christina said spying an outlet. The screen lit up as soon as Mimi called for her.

"Coming!" she hollered and ran to join the others. John had begun to take care of business right away.

"Roberto, you and Gabe stay here and file a report with the police while I head over to the Santa Bárbara mission to look around and make sure nothing else is missing," John ordered. "I'm going to stop by the Santa Inés mission too, and make sure everything's okay there."

"You wanted to see all 21 missions," John said turning towards Papa and Mimi. "Do you want to come with me tonight? I've got to get to Santa Bárbara right away, but we can take two cars so you can stop on your way over to get something to eat."

Missing Bells

Off To
Dinner

"I saw a pizza parlor on our way in," said Papa, winking at Christina.

"We'll go. Rosario, don't feel like you have to go with us," she added, patting the upset woman's shoulder.

"Thank you. I think I'll stay here and see what needs to be done," Rosario said gratefully. "But my girls can go with you, if they like."

The four kids piled into the back of John's Navigator, while Mimi and Papa climbed in the front. John got into Rosario's car and sped away.

Fifteen minutes later, they'd pulled into the pizza place. In five more minutes they had placed their order, and each person was sipping on an icy soda from the tall red glasses the waitress had placed in front of them.

"Mimi, tell us what happened," begged Christina. Mimi looked around the table at the four worried children, sighed, and said, "I guess you might as well know, or you'll be making up a far worse story from the bits and pieces you're bound to overhear."

Mimi glanced around the table, looking into the eyes of each girl, then ending with a serious look at Grant.

"Mission bells are missing," she said. "Vanished. Stolen. It's the second theft this week. There are no clues, and John's afraid the missions will have to be shut

Off To Dinner

Missing
Mission Bells

down until the case is solved."

"I noticed there were no bells at La Purísima," said Christina.

"That's right," said Mimi. "They disappeared two nights ago!"

"Which mission this time?" asked Maria.

"Santa Bárbara—Queen of the Missions," answered Mimi.

"That's the site of the famous twin bell towers," said Christina. Everyone looked at her, puzzled over how she'd know that.

"I was reading about the missions on the Internet before we left home," she explained.

They were still puzzling over why someone would steal the bells, when two large, steaming hot pizzas were plopped down in front of them. "Extra cheese, extra pepperoni," panted Grant, as if he was famished, which in fact he thought he was.

As soon as everyone was finished, Papa paid the bill and they all piled back into the Navigator. They arrived at Mission Santa Bárbara forty-five minutes later.

"Wow!" said Christina, admiring the impressive

Missing Mission
Bells

To Santa
Bárbara

Why steal the bells?

building as they pulled up to the front of the mission.

"This church's design can be traced to a book," said Mimi. "A Spanish reprint of an architecture book originally published in 27 B.C. inspired the design. It is patterned after an ancient Latin temple in pre-Christian Rome. The building suffered severe damage in a 1925 earthquake, but has been rebuilt to its original appearance."

"Santa Bárbara is the only California mission that the Franciscans still control," said Maria. "Franciscans are the priests. They held onto this mission all the way from when it was founded to the present time. All the other missions were abandoned as the land and property were taken out of the hands of the church."

Grant decided to stick with Mimi and Papa, while the girls went exploring on their own. As he followed Mimi and Papa around, he noticed what looked like a short, fat-ended iron club, laying on the ground. Nearby were several shoe prints similar to the ones he'd noticed before with the distinctive wavy line across the tread.

"What's this for?" he asked Mimi and Papa, holding up the club.

Papa and Mimi stared at Grant in disbelief. "You found a clapper!" exclaimed Mimi excitedly.

Mission Santa
Bárbara

A Clapper
found!

"What's a clapper?" Grant asked.

"It's the thing that hangs down in the middle of a bell that makes it ring!" answered Mimi.

A Clapper found!

A Clapper found!

6 HIDDEN GEM OF THE MISSIONS

Mimi told the kids that they could explore the mission a little longer while she and Papa found John and gave him the bell clapper.

"Thirty minutes and then be back at the car. Don't make me have to come find you!" she warned.

At 7:30 p.m. sharp, Christina, Grant, Maria, and Clara sat on the ground beside the Navigator, waiting for Mimi and Papa. Maria and Clara, who had both studied a lot of mission history at school, took turns describing the missions to Christina and Grant.

"Churches were usually connected to other buildings as part of a quadrangle," said Clara. "The center of the quadrangle, or square, was an outside courtyard, filled with gardens and paths and fountains. The church would make up one side of the quadrangle. Living quarters

A Clapper
Found!

Describing
The Missions

including bedrooms, a kitchen, and gathering rooms would usually be located down another side. The library, tailor's shop, study rooms, a winery, and anything else they needed in order to be self-sufficient would be part of the rooms along the four sides. The rooms connected to create a continuous structure where the *padres* could live and worship and minister to the Indians."

"All this space, and they all lived in one building? Curious," Grant said aloud.

"It wasn't just that the priests wanted to live together, although they did spend so much time at the church that it was convenient," said Maria. "It was also for protection from the Indians they ministered to and from some of the people who settled in the area but weren't always too well-behaved."

"Especially once Gold Fever broke out!" added Clara.

Just then Mimi and Papa walked up. "In my opinion," said Papa, "these missions are pretty awesome places to learn about history!"

Everyone nodded in agreement as they took off down the road.

Thirty minutes later, they pulled up at Mission Santa Inés, which adjoined the modern town of Solvang.

Describing The Missions

To Mission Santa Inés

The rolling hills created a lovely setting for the mission.

"This mission has been called the Hidden Gem of the Missions," Papa said, admiring the lay of the land.

Mimi turned to the kids and said, "John's already here. The mission is closed for the night, but he's going to let us in to see the church."

They followed Mimi and Papa down a path and walked through the open church door. Only a few lights were on, giving the place an eerie glow. Christina tipped her head upward as she admired the paintings on the wooden beams that crossed the ceiling.

"Those beams are made of sugar pine, hauled here from 30 miles away," said John. "The designs were painted by Indians using dye made from native vegetables."

"Look at this," Grant said, pointing to a statue in a niche in the center of the altar.

"That's a statue of Saint Agnes," said John. "It's believed to have been created by native artists at the mission."

"Some of the Latin missals and vestments in the museum here are even older than the mission itself," said Mimi. "Missals are music books on parchment and vestments are ceremonial garments worn by the priests," she explained as she walked back towards the door.

To Mission
Santa Inés

Art And
Artifacts

After they all buckled back into their seats, Christina asked Mimi, "Do we still get to visit the other missions?"

"For the time being, our plans are still on," Mimi said. "In fact, all four of you need to hop into bed as soon as we get back, because Papa said we're leaving *early* tomorrow morning to drive down to Mission San Diego."

Grant and Christina groaned loudly while Papa smiled.

"Papa grew up on a farm," said Grant in explanation to Maria and Clara's questioning expressions. "Papa's version of early means reeeeaaaaalllly, reeeeeeeaaaaaaalllly early!"

Papa just continued to smile.

Art And
Artifacts

Back To
The Casa

7 EERIE E-MAIL

That night before climbing into bed, Christina *finally* got to check her e-mail. Given the old style of the architecture, she had been afraid the house would not have the connections she needed to hook up her computer. When she mentioned it, Mimi surprised her by saying that even historic sites have to keep up with the times.

Christina's computer quacked, signifying she had mail. There was a list of knock-knock jokes from Mary, tales of the Girl Scout Time Traveler's Camp (that she was missing) from twins Sarah and Ellie, a long letter from Regan, a short note from Mom, and a picture of her new baby cousin Avery (from Aunt Cassidy) wearing a cute yellow ducky bathing suit.

She didn't recognize the name on the last message, but she double-clicked to open it anyway. What she saw on

Back At The
Casa

Checking
E-mail

the screen puzzled her:

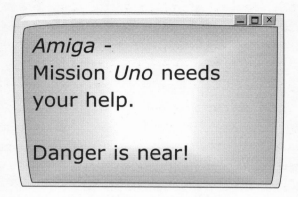

Amiga -
Mission *Uno* needs
your help.

Danger is near!

     Christina crinkled her nose at the strange message. Why did someone send her this message, and what did it mean? Was it even meant for her? Probably not, Christina figured as she looked up at the clock on the wall. She was so tired, she thought as she stretched out a giant yawn. Christina decided to think about it first thing in the morning. She shut down her computer and climbed between the cool sheets on her antique wooden bed.

     "Wake up, sleepy-heads," Mimi said, as she pulled open the curtains to a still dark morning. "Breakfast downstairs in ten minutes."

Checking
E-mail

Strange
Message

Christina rolled over and looked at the clock. It was soooo early, but she stumbled out of bed anyway. Grant was already squatting down in front of his suitcase picking out something to wear. He never seemed to mind getting up early, she thought with mild irritation.

They grabbed all their gear, knowing Papa would want to head out without delay. He would be impatient with them if they weren't ready to go right after breakfast. Papa had told them last night to plan on staying overnight at a couple of the other missions, but Christina couldn't remember which one he said they were going to see first.

Downstairs, a long banquet table had been set with freshly muffins, a big bowl of softly scrambled eggs, platters of bacon, link sausages, and carafes of fresh squeezed orange juice. Fragrant red and yellow flowers dotted the table in small white ceramic vases.

Maria, Clara, and their parents were already at the table when Mimi, Grant, and Christina arrived. Papa said a short grace, and then they all filled their plates with the delicious food. A young Mexican girl hovered nervously around the table, bringing more plates of food and clearing off the empty dishes. Christina recognized her as the same girl who had brought fresh fruit to their rooms last night. Christina smiled at her as she refilled their water glasses.

Time for
Breakfast

Let's Eat!

A pink and orange sunrise streaked sunrays across the room, lighting up the table and shining on the beautiful Mexican blanket hanging on the wall. Papa looked up and said in his usual gruff tone, "Time to go. Kids, grab your bags and get in the car."

While the adults filled their shiny silver mugs with steaming coffee for the road, the kids grabbed their backpacks and books, and piled into the Navigator. Mimi and Papa got in front, and John climbed in the middle next to Grant. The three girls squeezed into the back, with Christina in the center of the seat. They waved goodbye to Rosario.

"San Diego de Alcalá, here we come!" said Papa cheerfully, as they pulled out onto Highway 101.

The time passed quickly as the girls played hangman, tic-tac-toe, and other games in the backseat. Grant listened to the adults' conversation with one ear and the girls' with the other, all the while drawing dinosaurs in his sketchbook.

As they approached the city of San Diego, John told them more mission history.

"San Diego de Alcalá was the first mission founded in California. The missions were supposed to help the Indians, but so many Indians were killed by disease, the

Let's Eat!   To San Diego

missions were not always the blessing they might have seemed. The Indians had no immunity to the diseases brought by settlers and explorers. Of course it was secularization that really put an end to the missions. That and Pío Pico!" John said, with a distinct tone of anger.

"What is secularization?" asked Christina.

"In 1820, the war between Spain and her North American colony, New Spain, ended," said Papa. "New Spain had won the war and became Mexico, an independent nation. Mexico's government stripped California missions of their power over the Indians and took mission land and property as government property. The government then sold the property, often to people with political connections. The Indians were free, but frequently had no choice but to take jobs on the new Mexican-owned cattle ranches."

"Who's Pico Pico?" Grant asked hesitantly.

"*Pío* Pico took much of the mission land and property for himself and his brother once it was no longer protected as part of the church," answered Mimi. "He used his influence as a governor and grabbed up everything he could get his hands on. In fact, it's a wonder the missions exist today! The church lost almost all its land, and only thanks to later efforts have parts of the missions been

To San Diego

Who's Pío Pico?

restored or rebuilt so this part of history can continue to be shared."

Christina knew that Mimi felt strongly about preserving history and making it available for anyone to see or experience. It was one of her pet peeves when lessons from history weren't preserved and especially when they weren't shared truthfully. Mimi always liked to hear both sides of the story, as Christina had learned there almost always was. You could say truth-in-history was one of Mimi's missions, Christina thought, giggling to herself at her pun.

The ring of John's cell phone interrupted the conversation in the car. "Hello?" John said, pushing the green talk button. After a short conversation, he disconnected and said, "We've got to make a detour and stop by the King of the Missions before we go the rest of the way to San Diego."

"What's happened?" Papa asked.

"More bells have vanished," John replied. He slammed his fist angrily against the car door.

Who's Pio Pico?

More Missing Bells!

8 KING OF THE MISSIONS AND MISSION UNO

Christina jolted upright with the memory of the strange message she had received last night. Not wanting to alert the adults, she kept quiet but squirmed impatiently as they turned and drove the last few miles to the mission.

"Why is it called King of the Missions?" Grant asked John.

"Mission San Luis Rey de Francia became the largest and richest of all the missions. It's great quadrangle was 500 feet long on each side. An elaborate aqueduct system supplied water not only for the mission and garden, but also for pools used for bathing and laundry. Huge quantities of cattle, sheep, and horses roamed the *rancho*. Extraordinary quantities of bushels of grain and barrels of wine were produced. Once Mexico was freed from Spain and began to divide the spoils of the missions, Governor

More Missing Bells!

Mission San Luis Rey de Francia

Pío Pico and his brother alone appropriated (a big word for took) 90,000 acres of this mission's land for themselves."

"What happened to the Indians?" Christina asked.

"The U.S. government moved them to a reservation in Pala. They are still there and are still ministered to," said John.

As soon as the car pulled up to Mission San Luis Rey de Francia and the car doors opened, Christina motioned to Maria, Clara, and Grant to follow her to a little garden area.

"Kids, stay nearby," called Mimi as she watched the kids scurry around the corner."

"Yes ma'am," Christina called back.

As soon as they were away from the adults, Maria asked, "Christina, what's going on? Why are you pulling on me?"

"Last night I got an e-mail about the missing bells!" Christina blurted. "Look!" she said, pulling out a folded printout of the strange message and showing it to the others.

"Woooooooo!" said Grant eerily.

"Why didn't you tell us?" Clara asked softly.

"I forgot," said Christina meekly. "In fact, I thought maybe I'd received it by mistake. That's still a possibility.

Mission San Luis
Rey de Francia

Missing Bell
E-mail

What is going on?

Besides, I was so tired when I read it last night, and I just remembered in the car when your Dad mentioned the missing bells."

Maria looked at Christina skeptically, but Grant spoke up in defense of his sister.

"When she's tired, she really does forget things. Once she ate Papa's last piece of birthday cake as a midnight snack, and the next day she swore it was me. 'Course maybe that doesn't mean anything," said Grant, thinking about it a little harder.

"Anyway," said Christina, "I'm telling you now, and we've got to figure out what to do!"

The four kids looked at each other for a minute, and then Maria said, "Let's analyze the clue, line by line."

"Good idea," said Christina, spreading the sheet out on the ground. "The first line is *Amiga*. That means friend."

"That's better than enemy!" said Clara.

"Unless it's a trick," added Grant.

"The next line says Mission *Uno* needs your help," said Grant. "*Uno* is Spanish for one."

"Mission One–that's the mission in San Diego where we were supposed to be going!" declared Clara.

"We'll still go," said Christina. "Whenever we finish

Missing Bell
E-mail

Analyze The
Clue!

what has to be done here."

"The last line says 'Danger is near!'" said Grant, shivering. "I guess all that's left for us to figure out is *who* to help and *how* to help him or her."

Analyze The
Clue!

Danger Is
Near?

9 DANGER CLOSE AT HAND

Christina, Grant, Maria, and Clara spent the rest of the morning exploring the mission buildings. They wandered through the huge courtyards and quadrangle, pondering the mysterious message.

"Look at this," said Maria, peering at something on the wall in the mission museum.

"What is it?" asked Christina excitedly.

"This is the original decree that returned the mission buildings and a few of the surrounding acres to the church," said Maria. "It was signed by President Abraham Lincoln on March 18, 1861."

"That's neat," said Christina, "but I hoped it was another clue."

Soon Mimi came to find the kids and told them John had finished his business at this mission and they were

Danger Is Near?

Off To
Mission Uno!

45

ready to drive the short distance to San Diego. "Head to the car, everyone," she said.

After a quiet car ride, they arrived at Mission San Diego, the most southern of the California missions. The kids explored the mission on their own, looking for clues to help decipher the strange e-mail message. They found none.

For a treat, Papa took them to the San Diego Zoo–home to more than 4,000 animals. They returned to their cottage across from the mission at dusk and ate a quick dinner as they looked out the windows at the hard rain that had started to fall. After a dessert of vanilla ice cream topped with Ghirardelli chocolate, they were shuffled off to bed.

A few hours later, Christina awoke, startled by the sounds of loud voices.

"It's happened again, and this time right under our nose!" she heard John say angrily.

"Right above our heads is more like it," mumbled Mimi.

"I'll alert the authorities," said a man's deep voice that Christina recognized from the night before.

Christina looked over at her clock and saw that it was 2:16 a.m. She struggled out of bed and quietly padded

Off To
Mission Uno

Mission San
Diego de
Alcalá

down the hallway towards the voices. Mimi glanced up just as she was peeking into the room.

"Christina," called Mimi, waving her granddaughter over.

"What happened, Mimi?" asked Christina, tugging on her ear as she surveyed the tense mood in the room. "Why's everybody up?"

"More bells have disappeared," answered Mimi solemnly.

"From where?" asked Christina.

"From *this* mission," answered Mimi, putting her arm around Christina's shoulders and pulling her close.

Mission San
Diego de Alcalá

More Missing
Bells!

10 TOO LATE

Christina sat by Mimi for awhile, snuggling against Mimi's bright red robe, until Mimi sent her back to bed with a reassuring hug. Tossing and turning, she finally managed to fall back asleep, as the storm calmed down. She woke with a start to Grant kneeling on the edge of her bed, shaking her shoulders back and forth.

"Wake up, Christina. Wake up! There's been another disappearance!" Grant said pushing harder on Christina, trying to get her to open her eyes.

"I know, Grant. Stop. Pleeeeease. I'm awake now, I promise." Christina muttered.

"How do you know?" Grant asked, surprised.

"I was up for an hour in the middle of the night," replied Christina. "That's why I'm so tired."

"Mimi says the bells were taken from right

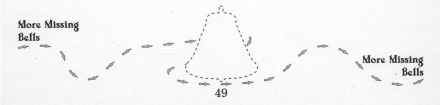

More Missing
Bells

More Missing
Bells

here–right here where we are!" said Grant with a nervous edge to his voice. "You know, right here at Mission Uno!" he added loudly.

Christina sat upright in bed.

"Yeah, we had a clue, but we didn't know it meant the bells would be stolen, did we?" she asked uncertainly.

Grant didn't answer. He was already getting dressed and shoving his pajamas back into his suitcase.

"Why are you packing?" Christina asked.

"Papa says we're leaving," said Grant.

"LEAVING? As in going home?" Christina asked worriedly.

"No. Not yet anyway, although he did mention it," said Grant, as he headed for the door. "Papa talked about going home, but Mimi talked him out of it. We're going to see some birds," he called over his shoulder as he hurried out the door.

Christina dressed quickly. She was glad she'd taken a shower last night—she would never get the chance if she waited until morning, what with all their early a.m. getaways. Christina hurried out to the kitchen, grabbed two slices of cinnamon toast, and sat down by Maria.

"Did you hear?" Maria asked Christina, in between bites of a banana.

More Missing
Bells

We're
Leaving

"Sshhh," Christina replied. "Don't talk about it here."

Maria nodded and concentrated on her banana while Christina ate her toast.

"Load up," Papa called ten minutes later, picking up an armload of bags and heading to the Navigator.

"I'm staying here, girls," John said to Clara and Maria. "I've got to finish up the police report today, and I'll meet up with you at San Buenaventura. You girls have a good time with Christina and Grant and be on your best behavior.

"Don't worry," he said, giving each girl a big hug. "I'll be there tonight."

Maria and Clara nodded and kissed their Dad before heading out to the car. Everyone piled in. Clara and Grant took the middle seats, leaving Maria and Christina with a little more room in the back.

"Bye," they all yelled. The kids waved as they drove out onto the main road.

"Capistrano, here we come!" boomed Papa.

Capa what? Christina wondered to herself.

We're Leaving

To Capistrano

11 EL CAMINO REAL

"Mimi?" Christina asked, as they drove the short distance north to Capistrano. "Why did Grant say we're going to see birds?"

"I know, I know!" cried Maria eagerly, as she bounced on the seat beside Christina. "Mission San Juan Capistrano is known as the Home of the Swallows. The little birds return every spring to Capistrano, where they build their mud nests among the stones of the ruined church."

Mimi nodded and smiled at Maria. "They return each year on or around March 19th–Saint Joseph's Day," she added.

"And the *El Camino Real* is going to get us there!" said Papa jovially.

"What's that?" asked Grant. "Sounds like a car," he

To Capistrano

On The El Camino Real

added before Papa could answer.

"Close, Grant," said Papa. "It's a road, although it was harder to travel on in the past than even today's Orange County Orange Crush traffic! *El Camino Real* means 'The Royal Road'. Many traveled the road to get up and down the coast of California, but there were long stretches that were unsafe because of Indian attacks."

"In fact," Mimi added, "five missions were built to help make the travel distances between stops no more than a day's ride on horseback. By building these missions, travelers would have a safe place to stop. Plus they could count on food and emergency supplies that they might need to continue their journey."

"If the Spanish were building missions to help the Indians, why did the Indians attack the Spanish travelers?" asked Christina, with a puzzled wrinkle across her forehead.

"Not all Indians thought being given the opportunity to live and work on a mission was such a great deal," said Mimi, nodding at the insightfulness of Christina's question. "The Indians who converted to Christianity found their lives changed a great deal. They were required to live in barracks at the missions. They had to spend hours every day in prayer and even more hours tilling the fields or

On The El
Camino Real

Indians &
Missions

tending the mission's cattle herd."

"Sometimes they were just scared because of all the deaths that occurred as the Indians contracted diseases such as smallpox and measles," Mimi continued. "The Indians had never been exposed to these diseases, so they had no immunity."

"So many Indians got sick and died, that whole tribes were wiped out," said Papa.

"That's really awful," said Christina. "It would be terrible if you were sick, and scary even if you weren't sick because you'd be so worried about getting sick. And, you'd be worried about your family and friends getting sick."

"Even today mission history is controversial," said Mimi. "Some people believe some Indians who did not convert to the faith and stay by the missions were mistreated. Of course, many of the *padres*, including Father Serra, had good intentions. They tried to further the goals of their country and to spread their faith."

Christina thought about what Mimi and Papa had said and realized there were many points of view to mission history. She supposed that no one really knew the whole truth unless they were there.

As she pondered the mystery of history, Mimi spoke up again.

Indians &
Missions

The Mystery
Of History

"I think I might as well tell you now," she said as they pulled into the drive at Mission San Juan Capistrano. "The bells here disappeared last night, too."

The Mystery
Of History

More Missing
Bells

12 Mud Nests and Muddy Footprints

The kids jumped out of the Navigator as soon as it came to a stop. Grant grabbed his backpack and hurried to catch up with the girls who had run off to get a good view of the bell wall. Open-mouthed they all stared at the empty openings where the bells used to hang.

"The *campanario* stands empty," said a voice from near the wall.

"Huh?" asked Christina, walking towards the sound.

"The *campanario*–the bell wall–it's empty," said a teenage boy who came out from the creosote bushes.

Christina stopped as the tall, lanky, dark-haired boy walked towards her. His left eye was black and blue and a fresh scab on his right shoulder gave him an intimidating look. He scowled at them as if they were trespassing.

"Who are you?" asked Grant, striking a John Wayne

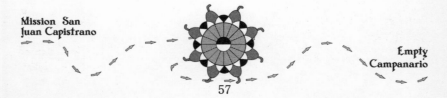

Mission San
Juan Capistrano

Empty
Campanario

pose as he bravely walked up to protect his sister. The other girls approached hesitantly.

"Miguel's my name. I live down the street," the boy replied, pointing over his shoulder at a desolate alleyway filled with trash. A black cat stood on a windowsill meowing.

"What happened to you? Did you get in a fight?" asked Maria, looking closely at the boy's injuries.

"Oh, yeah!" Miguel replied. "Last night about midnight there was a bunch of noise, and I came running down the street. I jumped over the fence and BAM! Something–or someone–hit me in the face and knocked me right back over the wall. I was out all night, laying on that prickly cactus right there. I woke up early this morning and the bells were gone!"

Christina looked at Miguel suspiciously. "You didn't see who it was?" she asked accusingly.

"No. I was out like a fly ball," Miguel laughed, as he turned and jumped back across the wall.

The four kids watched him walk down the street. When he disappeared from sight, they turned and walked back through the weathered adobe arches and past the ancient fountains that gave the mission such a feel of yesteryear.

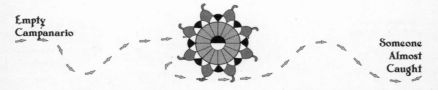

Empty
Campanario

Someone
Almost
Caught

"It sure seems sad that so much of the old church is gone," Christina said, looking around at the ruins. A single dome and few walls were all that remained of the old stone church.

"The earthquake collapsed the church, but it didn't stop the swallows," said Grant, scrutinizing the mud nests that the swallows built, crowded along the old stone walls.

"Hey, what's this?" he exclaimed.

Christina, Maria, and Clara ran over to where Grant was hunched down on his knees in the gnarled vines. "What is it?" Maria asked excitedly.

"Look at these big muddy shoe prints," said Grant pointing at the ground. "See that peculiar wavy line across the tread of the shoe? They're just like the prints I saw last night when I found the bell clapper!"

Someone
Almost Caught

Suspicious
Shoe Prints

13 ROOFTOP DISCOVERY

"C'mon," said Grant, motioning to the girls with his hand. "Let's go look for more mysterious shoe prints."

They walked along the walls inside the big quandrangle in a single-file line, looking for indentations in the mud. Christina was followed by Maria who was followed by Clara who was followed by Grant at the end of the line. Grant kept squatting down to inspect the ground, his knees caked in mud.

"I think I found something," Grant called near the corner of the building.

They all ran over to Grant, who had his hands squished into the mud beside a kiva ladder leaning against a tall stone wall.

"What is it?" Christina asked, trying to squat down without getting dirty.

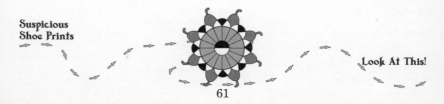

Suspicious
Shoe Prints

Look At This!

Grant's hands cupped three jagged pieces of muddy terra-cotta roof tile. "Look," he said, holding the tiles closer to the girls. "These broken tiles were clean before I picked them up. That means they must have fallen *after* last night's storm."

Christina and Maria nodded in comprehension.

"Let's climb up on the roof and see if we can tell what happened," Clara said. She grabbed the tall ladder made from tree limbs and started climbing.

"Wait," Christina called. "Aren't you afraid? It's really high up there."

"No, I take gymnastics and I have good balance," Clara replied nonchalantly. "C'mon guys, hurry up before someone sees us!"

Christina, Maria, and Grant all shrugged their shoulders at each other. When no one spoke up to object, Maria climbed up after Clara. Grant climbed next, followed by Christina who tightly squeezed the rungs as she peeked down every few feet.

Once on top of the roof they could walk easily along the gentle slope.

"Look," called Clara, still in the lead. "This roof connects to the section with the bell tower. Follow me!"

Christina bit on her bottom lip to keep from

Look At This!

Up Onto
The Roof

protesting, and they all followed Clara. She boldly worked her way down the roof.

Clara wasn't even afraid, Christina thought admiringly. How could she be so unfazed by heights, she wondered.

They reached the section where the adobe wall rose again and saw the bell tower.

Maria looked around and said, "There's more broken tiles up there," pointing to a damaged spot at the corner of the roof near the tower.

Grant strained to see the top of the tower. He looked up at the alcove above him, the levels built from the same material that formed the walls of the mission church.

"See that mud?" he asked excitedly, pointing to two long muddy streaks around the edge of the top opening. "It must have been made by the bell thief. It stopped raining last night about midnight, so the rain would have washed the mud away if someone had been up here before then. That means the shoe prints must belong to the person behind the thefts!"

"Yeah, and that person's been to all the same places as we have," Christina added, with a shudder.

Up Onto
The Roof

Mud & Broken
Tiles

14 MISSION SAN BUENAVENTURA!

"Maria . . . Clara," they heard someone call.

"That's Dad," Clara said with a startle. "What's he doing here?"

"I don't know," answered Maria, "but we'd better get down off this rooftop before he finds us up here. We'll be in big trouble if he does!"

The kids scrambled back down the way they'd come, Clara still leading, and Christina trying to keep up.

"I'm not really afraid of heights, but that doesn't mean I like running around on rooftops," she muttered to herself, as she finally put her feet back on the ground.

They took off running around the courtyard and through the nearest arched doorway back to the front of the building.

"Hey, girls," John said, reaching out to give Maria

What's He
Doing Here?

Better Get
Down!

and Clara a big bear hug. "I thought I'd meet up with you here before I head back home. I've got to get back to Mom, and then she and I will meet you at San Buenaventura, where we're all going to spend the night."

"Oh, good," said Maria happily. "I hate for Mama to be at home all by herself."

"Don't you worry, young lady," John said to his daughter. "Your mama is just fine. But she *will* be glad to see you."

"John?" said Mimi walking over with her hands full of books from the mission gift shop. "Would you mind bringing my computer with you when you come back down?"

"No problem at all," John answered.

Christina walked over to Mimi, looked up, and whispered in her ear. Mimi nodded and turned back to John. "John, if you could just bring the whole computer bag, that would be great. Christina is missing her computer too."

John winked at Christina as he nodded and climbed into the spare pickup truck he had borrowed from the San Diego mission.

"See you in a few hours," he said, waving as he drove off.

Better Get Down!

Back On The Road

"Okay *muchachas* and *muchacho*; you know the drill," Papa said, as he opened the Navigator's front passenger door for Mimi.

"*Muchachas*–girls and *muchacho*–boy," Maria whispered to Christina and Grant, answering the unvoiced question apparent by the looks on their faces.

Everyone climbed in, and Christina beckoned Grant to the back seat beside her. Maria and Clara buckled into the middle seats. As Papa checked everyone in his rearview mirror, he slid a mariachi band CD into the car's CD player. A lively Mexican hat dance tune filled the car. Grant, who loved to dance, began to wiggle in rhythm to the music like a Mexican jumping bean.

"Papa?" Christina asked, after they had driven for about thirty minutes. "Where are we going?"

Papa laughed.

"Why do you need to know where we're going?" he teased. "Don't you like surprises?"

"Yes, Papa. I love surprises, but where are we going?" Christina asked again.

Papa laughed even harder.

"Our destination for tonight is Mission San Buenaventura, the last mission established by Father Junípero Serra, on Easter Sunday in 1782. However, we're

Back On
The Road

Several Mission
Stops

going to make a couple of quick stops at two other missions on our way."

Christina felt better just knowing the plan for the day. She and Grant went back to whispering in the back seat for the rest of the drive. It was terrible that mission bells were disappearing. The bells were a beloved part of mission history. As soon as a mission was established, a bell was hung–often on a tree–even before the mission buildings were built.

But, no matter how hard she tried to make sense of the clue, the mud, the bruised boy, the shoe prints, and everything else, she could not figure out why someone would steal the bells. Mimi would say they were priceless antiques. But what would someone do with a whole bunch of old bells? It was a mystery to her.

Several Mission
Stops

Why Steal
Bells?

15 A PRICKLY SITUATION

"Mission San Gabriel Arcángel," Papa announced as he drove up and parked beside a tall mission wall.

Everyone got out of the car and looked around at the extensive grounds.

"Come on up to the church with us," Mimi said to the kids. "Then you can wander around outside on your own."

All the kids oohed and aahed over the intricate decorations in the church.

"The hammered copper baptismal font was a gift from King Carlos III of Spain in 1771," Christina read from one of the information signs. "These six priceless altar statues were brought around the Horn from Spain in 1791."

"The horn?" Grant asked. "What horn?"

"Cape Horn," answered Maria. "That's the ocean

Mission San
Gabriel Arcángel

What Horn?

route explorers sailed to get to the Pacific Ocean. They would leave Europe heading east and sail all the way down to the southern tip of South America. Then they sailed back up the coast on the other side. It was a long and dangerous journey. Cape Horn is famous for its fierce storms."

Grant and Christina looked back at the statues, even more impressed than before.

"Can we go outside?" Grant asked Papa.

"Sure," said Papa.

"Let's go!" Grant called to the girls, as he ran back to the front door and out into the misty gray fog that surrounded the church. "Ooooh, look! A graveyard!"

They took off running towards the ancient cemetery.

"Look at all these old tombstones," said Clara. "Think about how old the bones are in these ancient graves!" said Grant.

"It gives me shivers to think about it!" said Maria.

"Christina!" Grant hissed. "Look! It's that same shoe print I've seen everywhere we go! It's got that same squiggly line across it."

Christina squatted and looked at the marks in the dirt. "Are you sure?" she asked.

What Horn?

Another Shoe Print

"I'm positive!" Grant huffed, irritated that his sister didn't believe him.

"WHADDA YOU THINK YOU'RE DOING HERE?" shouted a crabby-looking man as he hobbled across the cemetery, shaking his fist in the air.

"C'mon! Let's get outta here," said Christina.

They took off in a run, but the man kept up with them. "WHATTA YOU UP TO?" he hollered.

The girls ran to the church. Grant ran inside the garden. He heard the man's feet scraping across the path, and he hid behind a large prickly pear cactus. The man passed him and hobbled to the other end of the garden. Just as Grant thought he was out of danger, the man turned and spotted him.

"AH HAH!" the man shouted as he scrambled to make his way back across the path to where Grant was hiding.

Grant fell back in surprise and shouted "EEEOOOOOWWW!" as his bottom came into contact with what felt like a hundred needles. He jumped up, and dashed out of the garden, leaving the man behind.

Mimi, Papa, and the girls stood just inside the mission church. Grant tumbled inside. His little face was scrooched up in pain.

Crabby Man
Chasing Us!

Grant, What's
Wrong?

"Mimi," Grant mumbled. "Help!"

"Grant! What's wrong?" cried Mimi, looking at Grant's tear-stained cheeks.

Grant spun around. Sticking out of the back of his shorts were a dozen long, sharp, cactus needles!

"Oh, Grant," Mimi cried. "What have you done to yourself?" Papa bent down and carefully plucked each of the cactus needles out of Grant's bottom.

"Ouch! Ouch! Ouch!" Grant squealed as each needle was pulled. Rubbing both hands across the seat of his pants, Grant sighed in relief. He peeked back out the front door, but the man from the cemetery was gone.

Papa looked puzzled. "Do you think that mean, old cactus is going to chase you down?"

"No!" said Grant, his feelings hurt. "I'm not afraid of a dumb old cactus."

But Grant looked afraid of something and Christina knew what it was.

"Back to the car," Papa said. "Grant, it's a good thing the next mission is close, so you don't have to sit down for long."

Papa quickly drove to the next mission.

"I'm only going to be a minute," Mimi said, as she got out of the car.

Grant, What's
Wrong?

Back To The
Car

EEEooooowww!

Papa sat in the car with the girls, while Grant got out and laid face-down on the grass beside them, still rubbing his behind and groaning.

"Mission San Fernando Rey de España was one of the missions added to close the gap between stops for travelers along the El Camino Real," said Papa. "The best spot was already taken by Francisco Reyes, Mayor of the Los Angeles *pueblo*. He gave up his claim to the land so the mission could be built here."

"I read that this mission was such a popular stopping place for travelers, that the *convento* wing was expanded again and again," said Christina, thinking back to her Internet research about the missions. "The hospice here became known as the famous Long Building *of El Camino Real*."

"Good memory, Christina," said Papa. "For awhile, this mission was very successful and wealthy. Livestock numbered in the thousands, and the mission produced hides, tallow, soap, and cloth. However, the Indian population on the mission decreased as new settlers arrived. Pretty soon, there were not enough Indians to produce the supplies that were needed. Father Ibarra remained as long as he could, but finally he was bullied out of the mission."

On To The
Next Mission

Mission San
Fernando Rey
de España

"Guess who got the mission's lands then?" Papa asked.

"Pío Pico!" guessed Grant.

"Correct," said Papa. "His brother turned the hospice into his summer home and used the quandrangle as a hog farm!"

Mimi returned to the car, her arms full of books from the mission gift shop. "Research," she said, smiling at Papa as she slid into the front seat.

A little later, Papa pulled onto a short drive that took them to Mission San Buenaventura, a mission smaller and plainer than the others they'd visited. From the street, its bell tower was its only distinguishing feature. Looming in front of them were two tall trees looking as out of place as antlers would on Christina's head. Grant hopped up and squeezed right past Clara to be the first one out of the car.

"Look at those trees!" he shouted pointing with both hands. "They're huge!"

Mimi laughed as she slid out of the front seat and walked over to him. "Those are Norfolk Island Pines," she told him. "They were planted by a sailing captain who hoped to grow a forest of tall trees to cut down so he could use their trunks as masts for sailing ships."

"Trust Mimi to know the old stories about ships and

Pío Pico Again!

Mission San
Buenaventura

captains and their crews," Papa said with a laugh.

Christina and Grant laughed. Mimi loved to write about pirates. In fact, Christina thought Mimi might have been a pirate if she'd lived in the right era.

"Look at the bells," Clara called from near the tower. "They're still here."

Mimi looked at Papa with a grim expression. Christina looked at Grant the same way. But how do we know the Bell Thief won't target them too, Christina wondered.

"You kids go explore," Papa said with his gruffness back in full force. "We've got to settle in and let Mimi get to her research."

Papa was very protective of Mimi, including her time and energy. If anything was bothering Mimi, Papa would charge in like a bull and fix the situation. So, Christina and Grant grabbed Maria and Clara with a quick "C'mon!" and hurried into the mission museum.

The kids toured the museum, then went outside and walked around looking for shoe prints, but they found none. They studied the bell tower but found no ladder, broken tiles, or other signs of mishap.

"These bells are made of wood," Grant said to the girls.

Mission San
Buenaventura

The Bells Are
Still Here!

They all three looked at him quizzingly. "How do you know that?" Christina asked.

Grant looked down at the information sign he had just read and realized he was blocking it from view.

"I just do," he said, shrugging his shoulders modestly.

A honking horn stopped any further discussion, and the kids followed the sound to the front entrance of the mission site. Mimi stood next to the Navigator, with the driver side door open.

"Get over here and get your luggage, kids," she called. "Papa's not a burro, you know!"

"Is that like a burrito?" Grant asked Mimi seriously.

Mimi laughed, despite her irritation with the kids for running off without unloading their books and backpacks.

"A burro is *not* a burrito, sweetie," she said, tousling Grant's hair. "A burro is a beast of burden, something like a small horse. Burros helped carry food and supplies the Spaniards brought with them as they explored up and down the coast of California. It was a long way to walk. Burros, donkeys, and horses helped make the journey a little easier."

Grant looked down at the luggage and grumbled, "I

The Bells Are
Still Here!

Get Your
Bags!

feel like a burro."

Just as they finished unloading their bags, John and Rosario pulled up in her green Chevy.

"Mama!" cried Clara and Maria, running over to give their mother a big hug.

"Silly girls," Rosario laughed. "You act as if you have not seen me for weeks. It has only been since yesterday!"

Christina looked over at John as he unloaded the trunk. She clapped her hands in excitement when he pulled out the computer bag, and she saw her laptop poking out.

"Mimi?" she asked in her most polite voice. "May I please take my computer into the house and check my e-mail now?"

Mimi smiled at her granddaughter. She knew Christina loved to use her computer.

"Go on ahead, if you like," she told her, with a pat on the back.

Christina picked up the heavy computer bag with two hands and carried it inside the guest house where they planned to spend the night. Maria, Clara, and Grant all followed her to the room she and Grant would share. Christina pulled out all her cables, plugged the laptop into both the electrical outlet and the telephone jack, and

Ooohh . . . The Laptop!

Checking E-mail

powered it up. She started up her e-mail program and typed in her password: S A V A N N A H. A few seconds later, she heard the familiar quack that told her she had mail.

Grant, Maria, and Clara leaned in close while Christina scanned the list of new e-mail messages. One from Ansley asking if she'd be back in time for her birthday party. Another from Dorothy asking if she was having fun. Rachel had written to tell her about the Girl Scout badges she'd earned at home while she was stuck inside, sick from her asthma. And of course, another note from Mom.

Christina was thinking what she might write back, when suddenly she spotted it. A new e-mail with that same strange return address. Slowly Christina moved her cursor to the unidentified e-mail and double-clicked.

What she saw on the screen confused her:

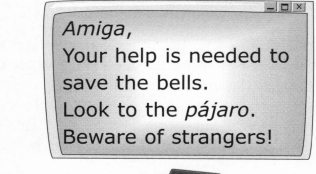

Amiga,
Your help is needed to
save the bells.
Look to the *pájaro*.
Beware of strangers!

Checking
E-mail

That's
Strange!

Christina moved over so Maria could read the note aloud to the others.

"That's really strange," Maria said, after reading the message. "It sounds as if we're supposed to help, but we're just kids. What can anyone expect us to do?"

Grant looked at Maria and Clara intently and said, "We get involved in lots of strange events when we travel with Mimi and Papa. You might not believe it, but kids *can* help solve mysteries. We know!"

"Sometimes the only way to stay alive is to solve the mystery," said Grant, remembering their scary adventures at the famous Alamo mission in San Antonio, Texas–where Jim Bowie and Davy Crockett had fought to the death–*their death*–to help Texas became a state.

"Well then, what do we do?" Maria asked Grant and Christina.

"I think we should start with your idea from last time and solve the clues line by line," answered Christina.

Grant ran down the hall in a hurry and returned with a small yellow rounded-corner Spanish-English dictionary in his hand.

"I borrowed it from Mimi's research bag," he panted.

"Help me remember to put it back," he asked

That's Strange!

A Little Translation

Christina, with a pleading look. They knew Mimi did not like anyone messing with her book-writing stuff.

"Ok," said Christina. "We know that *amiga* is friend, so we think this person is helping us."

"That's what we *think*," said Grant.

"What's this word, *pájaro*?" Christina asked, looking at Grant.

Grant handed the dictionary to Maria, with a quick "You do it." He moved back a few steps and sat down.

Maria looked up the word, but instead of saying its definition, she clapped her hand to her chest.

"What is it, Maria?" Christina asked.

"It's just as I thought," Maria replied. "*Pájaro* means bird."

"But that can't be," said Clara. "The bells were already taken from Capistrano, and that's definitely what I think of when I hear the word bird."

Christina scrolled back to the list of e-mail messages.

"Look!" she said, pointing a finger at the computer screen. "This message was sent last night!"

A Little
Translation

Birds?

16 DECIPHERING HISTORY

Christina pointed at the computer screen. "See!" she said. "It was sent at 9:55 p.m.! Someone gave us this warning yesterday, but I didn't check my messages," she added guiltily as she climbed up on her bed.

"It's not your fault," said Clara reassuringly. Clara climbed up beside her, while Grant and Maria sat on Grant's bed. "How could you have known? You couldn't have!"

"Well now I know, so I'm going to check my e-mail every day until we find out who's behind the disappearances," said Christina.

Suddenly, Christina's computer quacked. All four kids jumped off the beds and squeezed around the computer.

"What is it?" asked Maria eagerly.

Birds?

Another E-mail

83

Christina stared at the computer screen, then slowly turned to face the other kids.

"It's another clue," she said nervously.

"Open it, Tia," said Grant, using the nickname he had given Christina. He leaned forward as if he could decipher the contents of the e-mail just by getting closer to the unopened message.

"Yeah. Open it," urged Maria and Clara together.

Christina double-clicked on the new e-mail, and they all stared at the message that appeared:

> *Amiga,*
> Find the last mission founded by Padre Serra. *Madera* bells are in danger. Beware of *ojos* everywhere!

No one spoke for several minutes as they all read the message and silently pondered the grave warning.

"What's it mean?" Grant finally asked.

"Well, *padre* is Father or priest. And Padre Junípero

Another
E-mail

More
Translation

It's another clue!

Serra helped start many of the California missions," Clara reminded them.

"*Ojos* means eyes," said Christina. "You remember when I made *Ojos de Dios* at Girl Scouts?" she asked Grant. Grant nodded enthusiastically, and Christina turned to Maria and Clara to explain.

"It's a craft where you glue two popsicle sticks together, then wrap colorful yarn around the sticks to create a pattern. You use that yarn that changes colors, and when you're done it looks like an eye. Ojos de Dios means Eye of God."

They all nodded at Christina's explanation.

Grant said, "Eyes everywhere. . . that sounds like we're being watched!"

Clara shivered and looked at her older sister.

"We could be in danger," she said.

"Danger is probably right," said Maria firmly. "Why else would the clue say beware?"

"What about the other line?" asked Christina. "What's *madera*?"

"It's got to be in this dictionary," said Grant picking up the little yellow book and thumbing to M. "Mesa . . . madre . . . here it is!" he exclaimed. Grant paused to read the definition, then looked back up and said, "wood."

More
Translation

Wood?

"Wood?" asked Christina. "Are you sure that's what it means? I thought maybe it would mean stolen or disappeared or something like that."

"Well, I don't get it," said Maria angrily. "What are we supposed to do with this clue? Wood bells? What kind of sense does that make?"

The four kids lay sprawled around the beds and floor of the room, each in deep thought about the mystery they had found themselves thrust into.

Suddenly Grant jumped up and shouted, "Wooden bells! That's what the ones at this mission are made of!"

"Oh, yeah, that's right!" said Christina. "What are we going to do? We've got to stop the bells from disappearing!"

The others looked at her. "I don't know what to do," said Maria. "I'm scared, though. Let's go back to the mission."

Mimi, Papa, John, and Rosario were all standing in the parking lot when the kids got to the mission.

"Time for dinner," Papa said to the group.

They piled into two cars and drove to a festive Mexican restaurant a half mile away. They sat down around two big tables that had been pulled together to accommodate the big group. Baskets of warm chips and

Wood Bells?

Time for Dinner

small bowls of spicy red salsa and cool green guacamole were brought out and set on the middle of each table.

"It's really curious how this old mission sits in the middle of a busy town," said Christina at dinner.

"Mission San Buenaventura once included vast lands," said John. "A reservoir and aqueduct system, seven miles long, supplied fields with water. Land all the way to the shore of the Pacific Ocean was used for growing countless varieties of agricultural products. Mission San Buenaventura was very prosperous."

"What happened?" Grant asked.

"The Spanish king changed his opinion about missions," answered John. "Instead of wanting to build big missions supported by Indian labor, he passed new rules that missions would be churches only. His view had become such that he believed a few white settlers were of greater value than any number of Indians."

John shook his head in frustration as he continued. "Father Serra ignored the new rules for awhile, but eventually, with secularization, they were enforced. By 1845, all the lands–and even the church itself–had been confiscated! The church and a few bits of property were eventually returned, but the vineyards, orchards, and fields of grain were gone."

Time For
Dinner

Confiscated
Missions

"It seems really unfair that Father Serra worked so hard at building the missions to provide for the church and the Indians, and then it was all taken away and the church was left with nothing," said Christina.

Everyone continued to talk as they ate their delicious dinner of spicy tacos, quesadillas, beans, rice, and flan for dessert.

As they walked outside to the cars, Grant asked John, "What about the mission bells?"

"Don't you worry about the bells, Grant," John replied. "We've got guards out tonight to make sure there's no sign of trouble. Nothing's going to happen to Buenaventura's two old wooden bells. They're the only ones of their type in California!"

Not for long, worried Christina, as they got into the cars and buckled up.

Confiscated
Missions

What About
The Bells?

17 TRAPPED!

Christina and Grant whispered in the backseat of the car as they drove back to the mission.

"We have a clue! What do we do?" Grant asked his sister.

"I don't know," answered Christina. "I never would have thought we'd be in the middle of this mystery, but the disappearances are happening right under our nose!"

"More like right over our heads," Grant muttered to himself.

"Do you think the clue was telling us these bells are going to vanish too?" Christina asked Grant, already feeling the answer in her gut.

In the backseat, Grant nodded excitedly.

"Are we going to stay up and catch the thief?" he whispered to Christina, as he bounced on the seat in

What About
The Bells?

To Catch
A Thief

nervous anticipation.

Christina knew Grant was looking to her to decide what to do. She wondered if she should tell Mimi and Papa about the clues, but she worried that she'd lose her computer privileges that had taken so long to get. She was the only one of all her friends to have a portable computer, and she sure didn't want Mimi to take it away.

She had promised to be careful not to give out any personal information and to never go to web sites that weren't kid-appropriate. Not that she'd want to, she'd told Mimi and Papa honestly. She thought about how at dinner Mimi said a theft wasn't likely to happen again, especially with extra security patrolling the missions at night.

She decided not to tell the adults, but turned to Grant and whispered, "Yes, but keep it a secret!"

Back at the mission, the adults sent the kids to get ready for bed. Christina told Grant, Maria, and Clara to get into bed with their clothes on, and she set her clock for midnight.

Everyone fell asleep except for Christina, so she was still awake when her clock started beeping. She turned off the alarm, quietly woke Grant, and sent him down the hall to get Maria and Clara. All four were yawning and grouchy as they slipped out the door and across the street to the

To Catch
A Thief

Setting Up A
Stake-Out

mission.

"Let's set up a stake-out," said Christina, taking the lead. "Grant, you're the smallest, so you climb into the church through that little window. When you get inside, come around to the front and unlock the doors for us."

"Here, you can climb on my shoulders," said Maria, stooping beneath the small, high window. Grant climbed up on Maria and stuck his knee onto the window ledge. He pulled in his other leg, then crashed head-first inside.

The sounds of falling furniture clanged like pots and pans. The girls turned to see if anyone was looking. No one was, so Christina called to Grant, "Are you okay?"

"No!" said Grant.

"Good, then go open the door," said Christina.

Seconds later, they heard the sounds of large clunky metal locks being unfastened, and the thick wooden front door squeaked open a little.

Grant peeked outside and whispered, "C'mon in!"

The girls scurried inside and Grant shoved the door closed with a thud.

"I saw stairs earlier today where we can climb to the bell tower," said Maria. "Follow me."

"But I've gotta go," said Grant, pacing from foot to foot and glancing around for a bathroom.

Setting Up A
Stake-Out

To The Bell
Tower

"Hurry up," groaned Christina.

While Grant took off for the bathroom, the girls tiptoed one by one up the stairs to the bell tower. They stared up at the ancient wooden bells hanging above them.

"I still don't understand why someone would take the bells and not other more valuable artifacts," said Maria.

"Ancient golden altars and other treasures are left behind while dumb old bells disappear," she said, shaking her head. "What a dumbbell thief!"

Suddenly they heard a door creaking open downstairs.

"Quiet!" whispered Christina.

The *thunk thunk thunk* of heavy footsteps clomped through the church and started up the stairs. Maria and Clara looked at Christina in horror.

"In here," said Christina, motioning the others into a small storage room at the top of the stairs. Suddenly, the door slammed, knocking them inside.

"Meddlesome kids!" a man's mean voice hissed from the other side of the door. The clanking noise of a chain being draped across the door sounded deafening in the little closet. Slowly Christina turned the doorknob and realized they'd been trapped.

"Let us out!" she called. "We know you're stealing

To The Bell
Tower

Trapped!

the bells!"

The man laughed menacingly. "All the more reason NOT to let you out!" he snarled.

The three girls pushed and struggled against the locked door, but it wouldn't budge. They heard the sound of scrapings and grunts on the other side of the door, and the muffled clanging of the bells as they were shifted and lowered from where they hung.

A few minutes later they heard the *thunk thunk thunk* of footsteps back down the stairs. Seconds later the *slap slap slap* of lighter footsteps ran up the tower stairs.

"Christina! Maria! Clara?" Grant called.

"In here!" shouted Christina, as they banged on the closet door. "We're locked in!"

Grant struggled to loosen the chain from where it was wrapped around columns on each side of the doorway. Finally he loosened it enough to open the door about ten inches so the girls could squeeze out of the closet.

"I heard the man go up the stairs right behind you," said Grant. "I hid downstairs and listened to make sure you were alright."

Suddenly, they heard the creaking of the downstairs door being opened again and the pound of heavy footsteps coming back up the stairs!

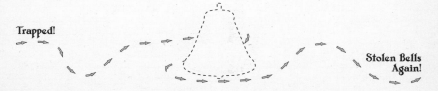

Trapped!

Stolen Bells
Again!

18 BIG TROUBLE

"What are you kids doing here?" demanded the stocky, uniformed security guard, as he reached the top of the stairs. The nametag pinned to his pocket identified him as Pedro Sanchez.

Christina sighed in relief to see that it wasn't the thief coming back to get them.

"We wanted to check on the bells," she answered honestly. "A man just stole them!"

Pedro Sanchez studied the kids, then looked up to the empty alcoves where the bells should have hung.

"Did you see him?" he asked.

"No," said Christina. "We were hiding in this closet." She pointed to the room they'd been trapped in just minutes before. "He locked us in here!"

"Look!" said Grant, pointing towards the floor. "That's

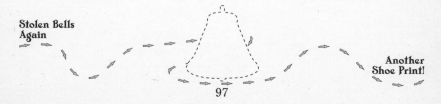

Stolen Bells
Again

Another
Shoe Print!

his shoe print!"

The security guard leaned over to look at the print clearly outlined on the dusty floor.

"How do you know this print belongs to the thief?" he asked.

Grant explained how they spotted the same distinctive wavy-treaded shoe print at the other missions.

"Did you show anyone?" the guard asked.

"We didn't think they'd believe us," Christina replied. "Besides, we weren't even sure ourselves."

"Let's go wake your parents," the guard said, as he started back down the stairs.

The kids followed and went to wake the adults while the guard waited outside.

John, Rosario, Papa, and Mimi all hurriedly dressed and went to talk to Sanchez. After hearing that the kids had sneaked out to check on the bells, Mimi sent Grant and Christina to bed. Maria and Clara had already gone to their room with Rosario.

"We're in big trouble, aren't we?" Grant asked Christina.

"Yeah, but . . ." started Christina.

"No ifs, ands, or buts about it!" interrupted Grant, repeating the phrase they heard frequently from their mother.

Another Shoe Print!

We're In Trouble !

The next morning, the mood was somber as the two families packed up their cars to leave.

Christina stared at her computer screen, wondering if she dared check her e-mail before she turned the computer off and packed it up. CHECK MAIL. She clicked, crossing her fingers that there would be no mysterious messages this time. Three new messages popped up. One from Mom. One from her friend Claire. And one from the unknown sender.

She opened the message, startled by what she read:

> *Amiga*,
> Danger abounds up and down the *El Camino Real*. Look for a man under a big *sombrero*. *Soledad*–NO!

"Oh, no," Christina groaned. She quickly printed the message, stuffed it into her suitcase along with the

We're In Trouble

Another E-mail!

computer, and ran outside.

Papa and Mimi climbed into the front seat of the Navigator, looking sternly at Grant and Christina in the back. They'd already lectured all four kids on the dangers of their midnight escapade. Not that any of the four needed danger to be explained!

Mimi looked over her shoulder and said, "We're going to continue our mission research, kids, because I'm going to finish the job I came to do. BUT, if I see anyone out of line, there's going to be big trouble for you two."

Christina and Grant nodded at Mimi, and sat quietly for the long ride planned for the day.

They traveled north on Road 1. Highway 101 would've been a little faster, but Papa liked to stay off the busier roads whenever possible. He and Mimi both liked to enjoy the scenery of all the little towns on the way to wherever they were going–even when they were in a hurry. Discovering and exploring the little nooks and crannies are what makes traveling fun, they always said.

Neither Grant nor Christina talked during the ride, but Christina could not get her mind off the mysterious note in her bag.

They pulled up at Mission San Luis Obispo de Tolosa at 9 a.m. When they arrived, there was no excited

Another
E-mail!

Mission San
Luis Obispo
de Tolosa

rush to get out of the car and explore as there had been at the other missions. They looked over at Maria and Clara as they stepped out of the other car. They clearly had their own lecture as evidenced by their glum faces.

Christina decided to keep the new message a secret. She and Maria went to explore the original *padres* quarters, which were now a museum. Grant and Clara heard the tour guide mention Valley of the Bears and stopped to listen.

"As Governor Portola and his men trudged northward in their search for Monterey Bay, they were surprised at the great number of bears they saw," said the young tour guide. "As a result of seeing so many bears, especially at the mouth of a small river, they named this region Valley of the Bears. They killed several bears for food. When they came back through this area, they brought 9,000 pounds of bear meat and generously shared with the hungry Indians. This kindness made the Indians much more receptive to Father Serra and his mission."

Grant and Clara followed the tour group and listened to more of the fascinating history. Then they heard Papa call their names and sprinted to the parking lot. Christina was already in the Navigator with Papa, and Maria was in the Chevy with her Mom and Dad.

"What's going on?" Grant asked Papa.

Mission San Luis
Obispo de Tolosa

Valley Of
The Bears

"John and Rosario are taking their girls straight to Mission Dolores," Mimi replied. "Grant, get in the car with us."

Christina turned and waved as they drove away. Just as the mission went out of view, Christina spotted a man in a *sombrero*.

"Will we see them again?" Grant asked.

"Yes," Mimi replied. "We're going to meet them at Dolores tomorrow night."

Grant told Mimi, Papa, and Christina how the area got its name Valley of the Bears.

Then Christina said, "This mission was the first to use terra-cotta roof tiles. Before the tiled roofs were used, Indians would set the old roofs afire with flaming arrows!"

"It's hard to believe that this one square block is all that's left of the City with a Mission," Mimi said as they drove off.

Grant fell asleep as they drove to Mission San Miguel Arcángel.

"I'll just stay in the car with Grant while you two do what you need to do," Papa said to Mimi when they got there.

Mimi and Christina strolled into the plain, rectangular adobe church.

Valley Of The
Bears

Mission San
Miguel
Arcángel

"Where's the bell tower?" Christina asked Mimi.

"There isn't one," Mimi replied. "This mission had no architect or engineer. That's why the church was built so plainly. But look at the insides of these church walls," she said in awe. "Indians decorated the bare walls with these intricate designs. This style of art is called fresco painting."

While Mimi went to pick out some books, Christina stood looking at the famous cactus garden. Her bottom felt sore just thinking of Grant's misadventures from yesterday. Too bad he's not awake to look for shoe prints, she said to herself. I wonder if the prints belong to the man wearing the *sombrero*?

When Christina and Mimi returned to the car, Papa was snoring away. Grant lay across the back seat so Christina climbed into the middle section. When they arrived at Mission San Antonio de Padua a little while later, Christina had fallen asleep but Grant was awake.

"I guess it's your turn to go with me," Mimi said to Grant.

"Okay," Grant whispered, as he climbed up to the middle seat and slid out the door.

"Want to see the bell?" Mimi asked Grant.

"Sure," said Grant. "Is it still here?"

Mission San
Antonio de Padua

Different
Bell

"Right up there," said Mimi, as she pointed to an alcove above the front door of the church.

"It looks different from the other mission bells," Grant said.

A man wearing a *sombrero* sauntered over to stand next to Grant.

"It's made of bronze," he replied.

Grant looked up at the man and smiled.   The familiar-looking man tipped his hat and walked away.

By the time Mimi and Grant got back to the car, Christina was waking up in the back and Papa was stretching after another short nap in the front seat.

Grant told them all about the bronze bell as they drove north to Mission Nuestra Señora de la Soledad.

"The bell was carried by a mule," he said, reciting one of the facts he had read while he was with Mimi. "It was hung from a tree branch where Father Serra would ring it, even before the church was built. A man came over and told me the bell was made of bronze."

Christina stared at Grant.

"This man. . . he didn't happen to be wearing a sombrero did he?" she asked.

"Yeah. How did you know?" Grant said.

"I've got to tell you something when we're alone,"

Different Bell

Mission Nuestra
Señora de la
Soledad

Christina whispered.

When they arrived at Soledad Mission, Papa said they could all get out of the car and spend an hour looking around. Grant put on his backpack, like usual, and they all walked together.

"No wonder it's called Our Lady of Solitude," commented Christina, referring to the mission's lonely, desolate feel.

"Sitting here, away from any nearby towns, this mission resembles the way it looked in early Spanish times, more than any other mission," Mimi said. "It's being restored, but it had fallen into such disrepair, that the restoration process may take awhile.

"The adobe buildings tended to disintegrate in this area's dry summers and wet winters," said Mimi. "It was a very lonely place to struggle to maintain a mission."

Christina and Grant wandered away from Mimi and Papa so they could talk in private. Christina showed Grant the newest message.

"That man was standing right beside me!" Grant said. "He could have killed me or something!"

Grant shuddered. He and Christina tried to think of what to do next.

As they walked across the lonely mission, Grant

Mission Nuestra
Señora de la Soledad

Look!

heard a voice coming from one of the remains of the deserted ruins. He looked over his shoulder and saw a hazy shape moving across the dusty, dry ground.

"Look!" he said, grabbing Christina's arm.

She turned in the direction Grant pointed, but the ghostly figure was gone.

Look!   Who Was
                                                                        That?

19 MISSIONS, MISSIONS, MISSIONS!

Rising at dawn for their last day on the mission trail, they piled into the car and headed northeast to Mission San Juan Bautista. There was a lot of tension in the car as Mimi and Papa discussed the most recent mission bell disappearances. Bells had disappeared from three more missions just last night!

"I'm worried it's not safe," said Mimi. "Maybe the kids should go back down to La Purísima while we visit the last of the missions."

"Noooo," groaned both Grant and Christina, not wanting to be left behind.

"No," said Papa. "We're all going to stick together."

They arrived at Mission San Juan Bautista, just as the sun was rising.

"Unknowingly, the *padres* who founded this mission

More Bells Are Gone!

Mission San Juan Bautista

built it directly on an earthquake fault!" said Mimi. "Even when walls of the building were split from top to bottom and giant cracks appeared in the ground, they rebuilt in the exact same treacherous spot. Another earthquake forced them to abandon part of the church."

"I don't think I'll go in," said Grant, wondering when the next earthquake might strike.

"Steel beams were hidden inside the walls to give the rebuilt church protection," Mimi assured him. "Even the bell wall has been restored."

Grant got out of the car with the others, grabbed his backpack and pulled the straps extra tight. He reluctantly followed to look at the famous original floor tiles and elaborate baptismal font sculpted by Indians from a huge block of native sandstone.

After San Juan Bautista, they went west to Mission San Carlos Borromeo de Carmelo.

"The Carmelo Mission is very unusual," Mimi said to Grant and Christina. "Its walls taper inward forming a catenary arch. They curve upward to form a center point. This mission was Father Serra's favorite, and now he lies buried under the altar."

They toured the mission and admired the stately stone buildings, but Christina and Grant saw no signs of

Earthquakes!?!

Mission San
Carlos Borromeo
de Carmelo

trouble.

The next stop of the day was Mission Santa Cruz where there was only a half-size replica built on the approximate site of the original mission.

"An earthquake and tidal waves destroyed this mission!" Grant read aloud from a brochure. "The California coast is some wild and crazy country!"

"The Spanish governor established a *pueblo* across the river from the mission," said Christina, reading over her brother's shoulder. "The *pueblo* became headquarters for gambling and smuggling. The *padres* could not meet the competition. The mission was headed for its downfall."

They got back in the Navigator and Papa drove on to Santa Clara de Asís.

"Where are we?" Christina asked, looking around at what looked like a college campus.

"This is part of the University of Santa Clara," said Mimi. "This section of garden wall is all that remains of the original mission. The university chapel is a reproduction of the old mission church."

"Bells!" shouted Grant, pointing to a bell tower.

"Those are the original bells sent from Spain long, long ago," replied Mimi.

Mission Santa
Cruz

Bells!

"We've got to make a detour to Mission San José," said Papa, turning off the road. "This was the first of the missions built to fill in the gaps between stops for travelers. Once the Gold Rush started, Mission San José was a trading place for the miners."

As they drove up to the mission, they heard music.

"Is it a fiesta?" Grant asked excitedly.

"Let's go see!" said Mimi.

They followed the melody to a group of Indian musicians dressed in authentic costumes of the mission era.

"They play here to demonstrate the music of trained orchestras that were started here in the early 1800s," said a short bald man who was watching the performers. "They played at fiestas, weddings, and on feast days."

There were 30 Indian musicians, playing flute, violin, trumpet, and drums. Papa and Mimi danced to the lively beat. Grant danced too, unable to resist the beat of the music.

"Olé!" Mimi and Papa shouted at the end of the song.

Christina laughed as she enjoyed the show. Her

Mission
San José

Olé!

grandparents sure didn't act like grandparents, she thought to herself. They could dance and have a good time and couldn't help but draw attention to themselves with their colorful styles and personalities.

They stopped for lunch on their way to Mission San Rafael Arcángel. "These last two missions were the last two founded," said Christina, looking at the numbered mission map she had borrowed from Mimi's research bag.

"San Rafael was the first sanitarium in California," Mimi said.

"Sanitarium! Is that like a planetarium?" Grant asked.

"No," said Mimi laughing. "A sanitarium is a treatment center for invalids. "The white man's diseases that the Indians suffered from were aggravated by the damp and foggy climate at Mission Dolores. Missionaries sent the Indians here where they thought it would be more healthful. The sunny hilltop location was named for Saint Raphael, the angel of bodily healing."

"Is that why they founded the last mission even further north?" asked Christina. "Because it was an even better climate for health?"

"Actually," Papa began, "Mission San Francisco de Sonoma–not to be confused with Mission San Francisco de

Mission San
Rafael Arcángel

On To San
Francisco

Asís which is in San Francisco and where we're staying tonight–was founded to keep the Russians out of California!"

"What?" asked Grant in surprise. "What Russians and what do they have to do with California?"

"The Russians had settled in the northern areas, up where the states of Washington and Oregon are located now," Papa said. "They were working their way south into California, trying to gain territory. It was a race between Spain, the United States, and Russia to claim and settle this area. Spain established that northern-most mission with the purpose in mind of keeping the Russians from moving south!"

After they finished their lunch, they visited the two missions and toured the reconstructed churches. Knowing they would meet up with Maria and Clara at Mission San Francisco de Asís, Christina and Grant struggled not to show their impatience to leave each site. When they finally got in the Navigator and Papa started driving south, everyone sighed in relief, even the adults.

Grant and Christina perked up noticeably as they reached the final mission and saw Maria and Clara out on the lawn waiting for them.

Grant and Christina slowly lugged their bags into

Mission San
Francisco de Sonoma

Russians?

the small guest cottage where they would spend the night. When Grant put on his backpack, it made a short beep. He unzipped the pocket, looked inside, and then zipped it back up. They went back outside and sat on the ground beside the picnic table where the adults had gathered to talk.

"Can I trust you to stay nearby?" Mimi asked Grant and Christina?

"Yes ma'am." They both nodded vigorously.

"And to stay out of trouble?" Mimi added.

"Yes ma'am." They nodded again.

"I know you are just trying to help," Mimi said turning to face them. "It's admirable that you are concerned about the safety of the bells. BUT, remember that *your* safety is more important than all the bells of all the missions, and while I know you've scraped through some pretty harrowing events in the past year, there's no point in putting yourself in danger on purpose! Now come here," she said, giving Grant and Christina a squeeze when they ran over to her.

"We'll be careful," Christina said to Mimi, wondering why Mimi did *not* look like she believed her.

"Very careful," Grant promised.

Mission San
Francisco de Asis

Stay Out Of
Trouble!

We promise we'll be careful!

20 DANGEROUS DOLORES

"What should we look at first?" Maria asked the others, as they walked out of the cottage.

"Nothing to get us in trouble," replied Clara.

The four of them wandered around the mission, looking at the ornate wall carvings, arches, and altar. They admired the decorated redwood ceiling beams that had remained just as they were created by the artistic and talented Indian workmen.

"Look at these Italian marble columns," Maria called out to the others. "They aren't marble at all–they're just wood painted to look like marble!" she explained, sharing the fact she'd just read on a sign by one of the columns. They continued to explore until Rosario called them all for dinner.

At the giant round table, they hungrily chowed down

Stay Out Of
Trouble!

Time for
Dinner!

on a delicious feast of fresh seafood. Papa and John continued to discuss the fascinating history of the missions.

"This mission is called Dolores because the *padres* founded it near the little inlet called Laguna Dolores," John explained. "The nearby *pueblo* was named Yerba Buena. Over time the names shifted and the town became known as Saint Francis while the mission became known as Dolores."

"Initially the Indians thought the mission was great," added Mimi. "Plenty of food and protection from their enemies made it a popular place. But after many Indians died of measles and smallpox, even the ones left were afraid to stay. That, plus the excitement and freedom offered by the nearby cities, caused so many Indians to desert the mission, that it almost became unpopulated."

"Nothing was ever the same after the start of the Gold Rush," said Papa to the kids. "The town exploded from 900 people to more than 20,000 in one year! It all started with the discovery of a little gold nugget no bigger than a dime. When Mexico ceded California to the United States as part of the treaty that ended the Mexican American War, they had no idea of the riches they were giving away!"

"Tales about the gold started spreading from *rancho* to *rancho*," John said. "All across the country rumors spread of gold in the streambeds, in dirt, under rocks, just waiting

Time for
Dinner

Dolores
History

for someone to come along and find it. Soon many people deserted their stores, animals, fields, and businesses to search for gold."

"Even schools closed so the teachers and students could go search for gold!" said Mimi, knowing the kids, especially Grant, would find this fact really cool.

"People all across the country heard the stories and imagined instant wealth," said John. "It was the end of a way of life for the Native Americans. They died from diseases, prospectors burned their villages, their families were murdered, and the mining process destroyed their food supply by killing the fish in the rivers and the trees along the banks. Approximately 150,000 Native Americans lived in California before the start of the Gold Rush, but less than 30,000 remained twelve years later."

Christina listened to the stories of California's history throughout dinner. It seemed so unfair to the native people who were here first, she thought to herself. But how do you stop change? Can you? Should you? Christina wondered.

After dinner, Christina, Maria, Clara, and Grant piled on the sofa in front of the big TV to watch a movie. By the time it was over, Grant had fallen asleep, and all the girls were yawning. Christina couldn't get Grant to wake up, so

Dolores History

Gold Rush!

Maria helped Christina carry him to the bedroom. Clara followed with Grant's red backpack that he took everywhere–even to watch TV. His backpack beeped as it had done several times that day.

When they got to the room, Christina looked at her blinking computer light indicating that she had new mail.

Christina helped lay Grant on his bed and then squatted down on her knees in front of the computer screen. She looked at the now familiar return address, and double-clicked. A new message popped up on the screen:

> *Amiga*,
> Dolores is in danger now,
> just as it was from the
> earthquakes, fires, and
> nearby *pueblo* long ago.
> Don't give up! This must
> be my last *carta*.
> Make your *madre* proud.

Christina read the message aloud. Grant stretched and rolled over on his bed.

"I think it's time to tell Mimi and Papa about the

Beeping
Backpack

Checking
E-mail

messages," she said, as she clicked PRINT from the menu and plugged in her small, portable printer.

Maria and Clara were nodding in agreement, when suddenly they heard a terrifying scream coming from the front yard.

All three girls jumped up and ran through the cottage to the front door and out to the *plaza*. They could now hear the cries for help coming from within the mission church. The front door stood wide open, but no lights shone from inside. They sprinted across the yard to the mission and ran inside.

"Hello?" Christina called tentatively, as the girls walked a few feet into the building. They didn't hear any screaming, but they did hear the sound of scuffling feet coming from the back of the church.

Suddenly, Grant burst in, his backpack across one shoulder.

"What happened?" he asked, looking at Christina in the dark.

"We don't know yet. but I think someone here needs our help," she whispered. as she took slow steps towards the grunts and noises ahead of her.

"Who's there?" Maria called out. as she walked beside Christina.

Checking E-mail

Who Screamed?

Just then a man came into view, his arm twisted around the neck of someone they recognized as the girl from Mission La Purísima.

"Run!" she cried, struggling under the grip of her captor.

Suddenly a high-pitched beeping came from Grant's backpack.

"Oh, no!" Grant said, frantically looking around.

"What is it?" asked Christina and Clara at the same time.

"EARTHQUAKE!" Grant shouted, as the beeping from his backpack screeched even louder. "This mission survived the Great Earthquake of 1906–hopefully it will survive today! Get on the ground and cover your head!"

The floor started vibrating, and the walls shook as if a 5,000 pound gorilla was jumping on the roof. A strange rumbling began low in the earth and grew into a deafening growl. Loose decorations bounced across the room and tiles crashed into sharp shards. It felt as if the earth were a quilt and a monster was flapping it around by one corner. Christina screamed!

The man tightened his grip on the girl he had in a strangle-hold in his arms and looked around for the nearest exit, panic on his face. He turned towards the side door and

Who Screamed?

Earthquake!

ran in that direction, pulling the girl with him. Just as he escaped through the door, another spray of tiles shot down from the roof, knocking him on the ground and cutting a wide gash across his forehead. A bolt of fire burst across the sky just outside the nearest window.

The horrible vibrations stopped as suddenly as they had begun. The man jumped up and was halfway across the yard, the kids running behind him, when a huge river of mud tore across the grass. As they all stared in fright at the oncoming mud, it roared over them like an avalanche of brown snow. Clara screamed and fainted. Maria grabbed her hand and held on tight.

Christina struggled against the unrelenting flow of mud and dug her way to firm ground. She snatched an iron pipe that the mudslide had ripped from a fence and dumped nearby. She held it out to Maria who grabbed the other end and pulled herself and the still unconscious Clara to safety. Urgently she reached the pipe out again to Grant who was choking on a mouthful of mud.

"Grant, reach out and grab hold!" Christina cried. "Please, you can do it! Try!"

Blinded by the mud in his eyes, Grant groped for the pipe. After two tries, he caught it in his grip, threw the other hand up to it and squeezed with all his might!

Earthquake!

Mudslide!

Christina pulled the pipe towards her, praying Grant's hands wouldn't slip off before she could pull him to safety.

When he got close enough, she dropped the pipe and reached down to grab him by a strap of the backpack still hooked across his shoulders. Together they crawled away from the gushing river of mud.

Christina looked around and spotted the girl, safely on the far side of the mud flow. She saw no sign of the man who had threatened them only minutes before.

Christina turned back to Clara and watched Maria shake her gently. Maria called out Clara's name and pleaded for her to wake up. Grant wiped his swollen, mud-filled eyes on his backpack as he spit out gooey wads of brown gunk.

Clara woke up mumbling. "What happened? What happened?" she asked, as her eyes opened wide in terror.

An eerie feeling came over Christina and she felt the hair on her head tingle. Slowly she turned from Clara to face the yard.

"I'll get you meddlesome kids!" sneered the man, so covered in mud that only the whites of his evil-looking eyes showed. He rose from the murk, picked up the iron pipe, and held it menacingly over his head. Slowly, mud sucking at his heels, he stalked toward them.

Mudslide!

OH, NO!

21 Hoax!

"Put down the pipe, Gabe!" boomed John's voice from the arched doorway, as he walked into the yard.

The man turned towards John, the pipe still raised threateningly over his head.

Papa and two police officers walked through the doorway, followed by Mimi and Rosario who ran over to the kids.

"Drop it and put your hands up!" one of the police officers shouted to the man. The man dropped the club to the ground with a thud and raised his hands.

While the police officers cuffed the man called Gabe, Christina asked Mimi how had they known where to find them.

"You can thank your brother for that," she said, reaching into her pocket and pulling out the printout of the

Oh, NO!

Got Him!

125

last clue. "This was stuck on the front door," she said, waving the paper which had a big "Mimi" scrawled across the top in Grant's handwriting. "I knew you kids must be back on the trail of the thief and that meant you'd be near the bells. Of course, I had no idea an earthquake was going to strike! It started right as we ran out of the house."

"Why did you do it?" John asked Gabe, before the police led him to the waiting police car. As he walked off, the kids spied his distinctive shoe prints in the mud.

"One of those bells is made of gold," sneered Gabe, "and I was going to find it!"

"I found this letter sorting through a bunch of old correspondence written by Pío Pico himself," Gabe said motioning to a tattered envelope sticking out of his muddy pocket. "I translated it and it says that in 1836 he and his brother melted down their gold and formed a bell. They covered it in lead and hung it in a mission. They planned to come back and recover the bell a few years later, but Pío died before he had a chance.

"This was my chance to get rich, but you kids ruined it!" he said, looking angrily at Christina.

John laughed then shook his head at Gabe.

"That letter is a hoax. Dozens of those were found twenty years ago. Most have been trashed, but you

Got Him!

A Pío Pico Hoax!

obviously found one that survived. Don't you think the missions would know if one of the bells was made of gold?" he asked.

Gabe shook in anger, mud clots falling off him in nasty blobs. One of the police officers pushed him through the doorway and out of view.

"Gabe worked at the missions," said John. "Usually he's at La Purísima, but he visits them all on occasion. He was in charge of upkeep of the grounds and buildings."

"But who sent the clues?" Christina asked.

"I did," said the young girl, as she made her way around to their side of the yard. "I work for Gabe, cleaning La Purísima and sometimes Santa Bárbara. And of course helping out at Señor John and Señora Rosario's house when they have business guests–that's where I met you."

"One night when I was cleaning Gabe's office, I bumped the computer and the monitor lit up. I didn't mean to snoop, but I noticed a list of missions and the number of bells at each one. When the bells started disappearing in the same order as his list, I knew they had to be related! I was afraid to come forward directly," she said, dropping her head slightly. "I really need my job because my *madre* has been very sick. We need the money I earn to support my mother and three young brothers."

A Pio Pico Hoax!

YOU Sent
The Clues!

"But why did you send clues to us? And how did you know my e-mail address?" Christina asked the girl.

"I overheard you all talking about the mysteries you had solved together. You seemed nice, and I saw your computer when I cleaned your room. I'm sorry, but it was easy to log on and get your e-mail address. I needed help, and I didn't know where to turn," she said.

"Juanita, I'm sorry you didn't know you could come to me," said John. "How did you get here tonight?"

"Earlier I went back into Gabe's office so I could log onto his computer and print the list I'd found. Gabe came in while I was there. When he saw what was on the screen, he realized I knew what he was up to. He brought me along, and said when I was found with my fingerprints all over the bell tower, the police would think I was the thief. I wasn't sure if I was going to be found dead or alive," she said with a shudder.

"Well, you're alive, thanks to the persistence of these kids," said John, looking around at Christina, Grant, Maria, and Clara. "Who would have thought they could solve this mystery?"

Mimi smiled knowingly. Kids solving mysteries? That didn't surprise her!

YOU Sent
The Clues!

Mystery
Solved!

We solved the mystery!

22 BELLS RINGING

Back at the house across from La Purísima the next afternoon, Christina and Grant walked into the big living room, pulling their suitcases behind them. Everyone had already gathered around the table for lunch when they sat down. A gray-haired woman came out of the kitchen carrying a basket of freshly baked sourdough bread.

"Where's Juanita?" Christina asked worriedly. "Did she get fired?"

"No," John laughed. "Quite the opposite, in fact. I've needed an assistant to help me catalog all the mission artifacts and relics. Juanita is quite the computer expert! I offered her the job, and she accepted right away. It's a great opportunity, and the extra pay will help out her family. Señora Bella is just helping out until I can find a replacement for around the house."

Mystery Solved!

Juanita Gets Promoted!

Christina sighed in relief. "Wow! I bet Juanita is really happy. I'm glad she got a better job."

Just then, Señora Bella's husband appeared in the doorway with a large pitcher of lemonade. He wore a big *sombrero*. Clara giggled.

"Well that explains that," she whispered to Maria. Both girls laughed.

"Speaking of really happy," said Mimi to the kids, "I know you will be happy to hear that the bells have all been recovered! Gabe hid them in one of the storage buildings where the mission workers keep tools for the gardens. Except for the one missing clapper, which Grant already found, all the bells are in fine condition. They are going to be re-hung today. There's even going to be a celebration of thanks at all the missions on Sunday. All 21 California missions will ring their bells at the same time!"

"I hope we can stick around for that," Christina said, giving Papa a pleading look.

"All that bell-ringing will surely wake the dead!" said Papa.

"Please don't say that!" said Christina.

"By the way, Grant," said Christina, "what did Uncle Michael put in your red backpack?"

"Yeah," added Clara. "And why did it start beeping

Juanita Gets
Promoted

The Bells Are
Safe!

so loudly last night?"

All heads turned toward Grant as he pulled the backpack off the floor and unzipped it.

"This!" he said, pulling out a black metal contraption labeled Eager Eddie's Earthquake Detector.

"Lifetime guarantee!" Grant read off the side of the machine, as everyone laughed.

The End

The Bells Are Safe!

The End

CALIFORNIA MISSION

Places To Go & Things To Know!

Mission La Purísima Concepción, Lompoc – destroyed by earthquake and then completely restored in 1935

Mission Santa Bárbara, Santa Bárbara – "Queen of the Missions"and the last California mission to be secularized

Mission Santa Inés,Solvang – "Hidden Gem of the Missions"

Mission San Luis Rey de Francia, San Luis Rey – the wealthiest Spanish mission, located between San Diego and Capistrano

Mission San Diego de Alcalá, Mission Valley – first mission

Mission San Juan Capistrano, San Juan Capistrano – founded by Father Lasuén and Father Serra; home of the mud swallows

Mission San Gabriel Arcángel, San Gabriel – near crossroads

Mission San Fernando Rey de España, San Fernando – restored mission is now a park on San Fernando Mission Boulevard

Mission San Buenaventura, Ventura – Father Serra's last mission

Mission San Luis Obispo de Tolosa, San Luis Obispo – first mission to use tile tools, founded near the Santa Maria River

Mission San Miguel Arcángel, San Miguel – beautiful frescoes

Mission San Antonio de Padua, Jolon – one of the largest restored missions; housed as many as 1300 Indians

Mission Nuestra Señora de la Soledad, Soledad – flooding and disease made this place the unfavorable mission among padres

Mission San Juan Bautista, Salinas – only original Spanish plaza left standing in California

Mission San Carlos Borromeo de Carmelo, Carmel – burial site of Father Junípero Serra

Mission Santa Cruz, Santa Cruz – mission looted by pirates

Mission Santa Clara de Asís, Santa Clara – original 1798 bell

Mission San José, San José – remembered for excellent music

Mission San Rafael Arcángel, San Rafael – helped sick Indians

Mission San Francisco de Sonoma – last mission built

Mission San Francisci de Asís (Mission Dolores), San Francisco – original church still stands unharmed by man or nature

Historic missions can also be found in many other states, including Arizona, New Mexico, Texas, Florida, and Georgia.

ABOUT THE AUTHOR

Carole Marsh is an author and publisher who has written many works of fiction and non-fiction for young readers. She travels throughout the United States and around the world to research her books. In 1979 Carole Marsh was named Communicator of the Year for her corporate communications work with major national and international corporations.

Marsh is the founder and CEO of Gallopade International, established in 1979. Today, Gallopade International is widely recognized as a leading source of educational materials for every state and many countries. Marsh and Gallopade were recipients of the 2002 Teachers' Choice Award. Marsh has written more than 13 Carole Marsh Mysteries™. Years ago, her children, Michele and Michael, were the original characters in her mystery books. Today, they continue the Carole Marsh Books tradition by working at Gallopade. By adding grandchildren Grant and Christina as new mystery characters, she has continued the tradition for a third generation.

Ms. Marsh welcomes correspondence from her readers. You can e-mail her at carole@gallopade.com, visit the carolemarshmysteries.com website, or write to her in care of Gallopade International, P.O. Box 2779, Peachtree City, Georgia, 30269 USA.

SPANISH GLOSSARY

adobe: *(uh doe bee)* sun-dried bricks of adobe clay

amigo/amiga: *(uh me go)* male friend/female friend

burro: *(burr-o)* beast of burden

carta: *(cart uh)* letter

casa: *(kah sah)* house

convento: *(con vent o)* hospital

El Camino Real: The King's Highway, The Royal Road

fiesta: *(fee es tah)* party, celebration, holiday

hacienda: *(ha see en dah)* large ranch

madera: *(mah dee rah)* wood

madre: *(mah dray)* mother

muerto: *(mwer toe)* dead

ojos: *(oh yos)* eyes

padre: *(pah dray)* father, priest

pájaro: *(pah yar o)* bird

presidio: *(pray sidee-o)* military location/fort

pueblo: *(pweb low)* town

rancho: *(ranch o)* ranch

soledad: *(so luh dad)* solitude, all alone

sombrero: *(som brer oh)* hat with a wide brim

SCAVENGER HUNT!

Recipe for fun: Read the book, take the tour, find the items on this list and check them off! (Hint: Look high and low!!) *Teachers: you have permission to reproduce this form for your students.*

__1. First Mission (also the most southern)

__2. Mission that survived the 1806 disasters

__3. Mud nests of swallows

__4. Queen of the Missions

__5. King of the Missions

__6. First mission to use roof tiles

__7. Six altar statues sailed around Cape Horn

__8. Santa Clara College

__9. Father Junípero Serra's grave

__10. Grizzly bears

WRITE YOUR OWN MYSTERY!

Make up a dramatic title!

You can pick four real kid characters!

Select a real place for the story's setting!

Try writing your first draft!

Edit your first draft!

Read your final draft aloud!

You can add art, photos or illustrations!

Share your book with others and send me a copy!

Six Secret Writing Tips from Carole Marsh!

WOULD YOU MYSTERIES LIKE TO BE A CHARACTER IN A CAROLE MARSH MYSTERY?

If you would like to star in a Carole Marsh Mystery, fill out the form below and write a 25-word paragraph about why you think you would make a good character! Once you're done, ask your mom or dad to send this page to:

Carole Marsh Mysteries Fan Club
Gallopade International
P.O. Box 2779
Peachtree City, GA 30269

My name is: _____

I am a: ____boy ____ girl   Age: _____

I live at: _____

City: _____   State:____   Zip code: _____

My e-mail address: _____

My phone number is: _____

_____
_____
_____
_____
_____
_____
_____
_____
_____
_____
_____

Enjoy this exciting excerpt from

THE MYSTERY OF THE CHICAGO DINOSAURS

1 BEACH DREAMS

"One plus two plus eight plus one equals twelve," Grant said to himself. It was the last day of first grade and Grant was counting the hours until he hit the ocean waves with his brand new boogie board. He was pretty good at math even though it was not his favorite subject, but he decided to count the hours up one more time just to be sure. One hour until the bell rings, two hours until the car is loaded and his family gets on the road, eight hours to drive to Florida to their hotel, and one hour (or less!) until the car was unpacked and his Dad took him out to the beach! "Yep, that's twelve," Grant told himself.

Grant had been anxiously waiting all year for this

trip. For Christmas, he had gotten a brand new boogie board from Mimi and Papa, his grandparents, and he couldn't wait to get out in the water and ride the waves with it. It was dark blue with lightning bolts down the sides and was sure to be the coolest board on the beach.

"BRRRIIINNNGGG!" the bell blared and startled Grant out of his daydreams. "Down to eleven hours now," he said out loud.

"What's eleven?" his friend Wingho asked.

"Eleven hours until I'm shredding some waves on my board," Grant told him.

"Well, have fun and call me when you get back so I can beat you again in soccer," Wingho said with a laugh.

"Ohhh-kay," Grant yelled over his shoulder. as he ran out the door to catch his bus home. He zigzagged all the way to the bus, yelling goodbyes to all the friends and teachers that he passed. As he climbed the steps to the bus he saw a familiar face in the very front seat.

"Grant, sit here!" his sister yelled. Christina was as excited as Grant about this beach trip. Even though she was not into boogie boarding, she did love swimming in the waves and she especially loved all the great seafood that they got to eat at the beach!

"Eleven hours," Grant said in a matter of fact tone to Christina.

"Eleven what?" she asked.

"In eleven hours, yours truly will be hitting the beach and using my new boogie board," he told her smugly.

"Actually, you won't," she informed him even more smugly. "Because in eleven hours it will be two o'clock in the morning, and I don't think Mom and Dad are gonna let you swim in the dark."

"Aw shucks," Grant moaned. "It will be harder to sleep tonight than on Christmas Eve. I hope Dad is ready to get up early, because I want to be the first one on the beach in the morning."

Grant spent the rest of the ride pouting over his math miscalculations, while Christina chatted with her friends about hanging out at the pool for the rest of the summer once she got back from the beach.

"Get off, slowpoke!" Christina said, as she elbowed Grant out of the seat. "We're home."

They both rushed off the bus waving goodbyes to their friends and the driver and raced down the driveway. The anticipation of leaving for the beach had them both so excited that Grant didn't even care that Christina beat him to the door. He just wanted to grab his suitcase and boogie board and help Dad pack the car so they could hurry up and leave.

As they both plowed though the doorway they were quite surprised to find Mom sitting on the couch with tears in her eyes. Dad had his arm wrapped around her, trying to comfort her.

"Hey Mom. Hey Dad." Christina said, as she dropped her bookbag and ran into the living room. "What's wrong? Why aren't you packing the car?"

"It's only eleven hours plus one night's sleep until I hit the beach," Grant reminded them.

"Well, kids," Dad said slowly. "I have some bad news. We aren't going to Florida anymore. We have to cancel the trip."

"What? You can't be serious!" Christina shouted, not sure whether to be angry or start crying.

"Why can't we go?" Grant asked, hoping it must be a joke that his Dad was playing on him.

"Kids, I know how much you were looking forward to this vacation, but now we have to go to Chicago," their father told them.

Grant and Christina still didn't understand. Chicago? Why? They looked at their mother for an explanation.

"I have some really bad news," she said between sobs. "Your Uncle Michael has been kidnapped!"

THE CAROLE MARSH MYSTERIES SERIES

CAROLE MARSH MYSTERIES

Visit the Carole Marsh Mysteries Website

www.carolemarshmysteries.com

- *Check out what's coming up next! Are we coming to your area with our next book release? Maybe you can have your book signed by the author!*

- *Join the Carole Marsh Mysteries Fan Club!*

- *Apply for the chance to be a character in an upcoming Carole Marsh Mystery!*

- *Learn how to write your own mystery!*